T0208405

# This Love Thang

# This Love Thang

## Toki Swan

**To order additional copies of this book, contact:**
Xlibris
844-714-8691
www.Xlibris.com
Orders@Xlibris.com
814268

# CONTENTS

## STORY BREAK

# CHARACTER LIST

**PARIS:** A lawyer and aspiring poet who struggles to find love. Is she ready for the consequences of his actions?

**LEON:** A momma's boy who blames women for all the failures in his life, he was never taught to take responsibility for his actions. Did he go too far this time?

**TAMEKO:** Paris's best friend who lives her life destructively and foolishly all the while failing to make good decisions. Is it too late to turn back time?

**ALANNA:** An IBM executive who is so focused on building her career. Knowing her sister's history, is it smart to leave her man home with her all the time? A thin line between a sister's love and the man you want.

**JENNIFER:** Alanna's sister. The promiscuous one. Is she aware of all her behaviors toward the opposite sex? Is she is really incapable of comprehending her actions?

**EGYPT:** Married, educated, and loves her family, but will her own curiosity kill the cat?

**IAN:** Egypt's husband; he loves his family but lacks the listening skills his wife needs. Will his inability to listen cost him the most important jewel of his life?

**JOH ALLEN TOMAY:** He played his position well; she could have not asked for a better man, or so she thought. Will his betrayal force her to see what lies beneath?

**MASSAI:** The gangster lover; every good girl wants a bad boy. However, inside his concrete wall of silence, there is no place to run, the streets are not the same, and it almost devoured him. Will he get another chance at love? Is he ready?

**BRIAN:** Greed consumed him, and suddenly there were two women he wanted. He isn't ready for what lies ahead. He is a walking nightmare.

**SAMANTHA:** The best-kept secret that no one saw coming.

# FOREWORD

Love! The journey begins with you. How you love yourself teaches someone else how to love you back. Never fault yourself for what love has taught you and for having the courage because life permits it. Your standards are warranted and necessary because there is a bittersweet road to finding and accepting love. While the emotional rollercoaster of love takes us for a ride. Eventually, life teaches you how to love yourself through it all. Love is possible. **This Love Thang**—many will come to know it, and some will never know it at all, but the ones who dare to have it are often surprised by its results!

May you find something here that helps you on your journey from the moment you read it and embrace it and forces you to accept what it has revealed to you!

# DEDICATIONS

DEDICATIONS

To my Heavenly Father, who dwells within me.
The ultimate sacrifice for my life will never be forgotten. A
debt, I could never repay is my total commitment to your
word! You are the truth, the way, and my light, knowing
nothing comes to me but through you. Thank you!

Berra Jean Swan
1947–2000
(MOM)

I dedicate this book to you because you are the strongest woman I know, knew, and love! You gave me the desire to want more, and you showed me what true strength is all about. MOM, you taught me to keep going even when the road at times seem unbearable and full of obstacles. Mommy, there was never a moment when I was not proud of you or did not care for your well-being. I just wished I could have done more. I wish for one more kiss, placing them on those cheeks where my tears and kisses nestled.

I noticed how you took the time to show other people and their children unconditional love, all the while keeping an eye on all of us; it was a true testament to your motherhood. In the interim, you continued to give so much of yourself while never really receiving appreciation or gratitude for the beautiful woman you are. Absolutely astonishing to me!

I understood you when you thought I did not. I could not have wanted a better friend, sister, and mother. You are and were an amazing woman. Your faith, strength, and courage were unparalleled as it lives in me forever. In the end, all of what you gave me helped me to write this book. Thank you for being a blessing in my life. You were and always be our mom, knowing you did your absolute best. I love you always and in the end, you were a wonderful grandmother to all our children.

Your daughter,
Toki

## CHAUNTE
My daughter

They say, "the relationship between mother and son is uncanny, but the relationship between mother and daughter is priceless." Baby girl, you are the wind beneath my wings, and every breath I have taken over the years is for you. You are absolutely- beautiful, if I did not do anything right, the moment I became your mom—it was right. GOD wanted you to vessel through me, thank you for choosing me to be your mother. I have loved and wanted you from the moment you were born. You take my breath away every time I see you!

Chaunte, When I am stuck, you show up in my face, in my mind, and you hug me; it gives me the strength knowing I can do it all over again. Thank you for never letting me give up, and reminding me that I can do more and to keep moving forward. You are a mother's greatest gift and my proudest moment.

Never doubt yourself. You are an amazing, strong, intelligent young woman, and when I look at you, I did well. I love you with my whole heart, and I am so proud at how of an amazing mother you are! Remember who you are, and do not let them dictate who you are— Queen, you just are! I am honored to be your MOM.

Yours,
Mom

<u>My grandson</u>
<u>London</u>

The moment your mother gave you to me, I was in love. There is no greater love than that of grandchildren. We get to do it all over again and better. I live to laugh, play in the mud, play cards, run, and smile with you. "Who are you?" Know this always! It is your birthright! Because when I look at you, I see greatness! Remember, "a man who thinketh can have it." I love you to the moon and back and all the air in between. My first little king.

Love you,
<u>Ya-Ya</u>

## My Siblings

My mother raised several children, and we all consider ourselves sisters and brothers. I love each one of you with all that I am. We have had a lot of love and tears together, and we are still standing! Without you, my path would have been lonely. I am so proud of you all.

## Nieces, Nephews, and Greats

I am so happy to be a part of all your lives. I love being an aunty, and I love having a relationships with all of you; you are all important to me. Family is everything and no matter whose family you end up in, it's yours! Cherish the relationships you have with one another, and work harder to build better ones.

The Swan Family Dynasty!

# THANK YOU

**Barack and Michelle Obama**
*For giving the world YOU, showing us what following your destiny looks like.*
**Oprah Winfrey**
*Thank you for choosing me to sit next to you on your couch.*
**Cicely Tyson**
*Thank you for allowing me to still admire your dedication and hard work.*
**Tyler Perry**
*For allowing me to write along with you in creating the next masterpiece, cheers!*
**Ellen DeGeneres**
*Thank you for giving me the opportunity to dance with you.*
**Ava DuVernay:**
*I knew one day we would write together in the same space.*
**Wendy Williams**
*I knew one day we would have this conversation.*
**The Voice**
*Thank you. It's an honor to sit at your table, OMG!*
**BET Awards**
*Thank you, Ms. Lee. I've waited a long time to present this award.*
**Issa Rae**
*Your laughter is infectious.*

**Fantasia**
*Thank you for allowing me to write that song for you.*
**Steve Harvey Morning Show**
*Thank you for speaking truth to me.*

# ACKNOWLEDGEMENT

**The lost ones**
*For all the ones who have come and gone, I miss you dearly!*
**Berra Jean Swan (Mom)**
*For giving me the desire to want more.*
**My little sister, Terry**
*You keep me pushing every day. What is your next project?*
**My little brother, Tony**
*Thank you for always being there no matter what.*
**Tony Sales of Xlibris publishing**
*Thank you for your continuous calls.*
**Diane Dennis (Lady-Di)**
*Thank you for gracing me with genuine love. You make my heart smile.*
**Mr. Ronald Colbert Sr. (Mr. Rolo)**
*You were always my greatest supporter. I finally finished it. May you always shine down upon me!*
**Anitra and Christine, Felicia, Quinetta, Corrin, Tiki, Wanda W., Tony G., Cinda, and Hans**, *you were the first to purchase and my greatest supporters.*
**My new and old friends**
*Thank you for always showing up for me.*
*To every person, employer, director, supervisor, and colleague, thank you. If it weren't for you, I wouldn't have pushed myself harder. I am so grateful for all your encounters. I made it through!*

To my audience:

May you find a poem that resembles your heart. May you cry, laugh, and smile at the conversations awaiting you. *This Love Thang* is a journey to understand your path in finding love.

# GIRL TALK

*Is that my door? I know there isn't someone knocking at* my *door at this time of night. It's after 9:00 p.m.*

Paris begins to reset her mind back to reality. *Am I dreaming? Paris, wake your ass up!* she yelled inside her mind. *I hate when I fall into these deep sleeps, it causes my mind to drift back to yesterday's past. A place where I rarely want to go, but my mother is there now. She has passed on, and I miss her so much.*

*There it goes again. Shit—somebody is knocking at my door. I thought I heard someone.* Paris jumps up out of bed.

"Who is it?" Paris yells. "Who is it?"

*I know . . . I'm not imagining things, but then again, who could possibly be knocking at my door . . . at this hour? Shit, it's after nine o'clock in the evening.*

"It's me!" A voice shouts back. "Paris, open the damn door! You know who this is. It's me . . . Tameko! Who else would be ringing your door at this hour? *Paris acts like she old, but it's only 9:00 p.m. It's not like she has all this company.* Tameko thinks. *Open the damn door!*

Paris knew she recognized that crazy-ass voice, but she had thought Tameko would be still out of town. *Why would she be here after only two days?* Paris thinks to herself, but before Paris could walk out the room, he yells "Bae, who is that? Didn't I tell you about having company?"

"I am not sure. It is probably one of my friends. I . . ."

He looks over at Paris to say get rid of them. "I don't like people showing up unannounced. You know this!"

1

"His house? I know, babe, wait a minute, I will."

"Listen, you better or I will. I don't like people showing up at my house after a certain time. Whoever it is . . . they should have called first. Get rid of them, now!" the voice states.

"Stay here in the bedroom. Sorry! I wasn't expecting anyone either!" Paris shakenly states as she walks out of the bedroom. "I'll be right back," Paris says under her breath.

"What's taking her so long? It's cold out here. Paris, are you in there?" Tameko yells in the door.

"I AM COMING . . . BE EASY!" Paris yells back.

"REALLY!" Tameko answers.

"Who told you to bring your ass up to my house anyway? Security is supposed to get a call me for before anyone comes upstairs."

"I don't know why we're having to the whole conversation outside your door. OPEN UP THE DOOR, GIRL!" Tameko yells.

Paris shouts back as she walks toward the door, "I PAY TOO MANY FEES TO BE LETTING PEOPLE JUST COME UP IN HERE WITHOUT NOTICE. WHERE'S THE DAMN DOORMAN ANYWAY?"

"First of all—why are you yelling? I am not just anybody. *And* . . . no, he was not sitting at the desk. So . . . I just came up on my own." Tameko says, still talking loudly through the door. "Maybe he took a bathroom break. Shit, he's allowed. Dang girl! What's your problem? We girls. Why are you talking to me like you just met me? Besides . . . he knows me. He's seen me, noticed me, and, *hell—I think he likes me,*" Tameko shouts back.

"You think everybody likes you, Tameko," Paris replies.

"LET ME IN!" Tameko says, banging on the door. "Why am I still standing in the hallway? You got me standing out here like some stranger you never met." She bangs on the door again.

"Tameko . . . STOP BANGING ON MY DOOR . . . I'M COMING! I AM NOT DRESSED."

"HOW LONG DOES IT TAKE YOU TO GET DRESSED? Open the damn door," Tameko yells in.

You think everybody likes you . . . girl, that man ain't even thinking about you. He's *got* a woman! Paris replies.

"Honestly, I forgot about the doorman a whole fifteen minutes ago. I don't understand what's taking you so long. It's a door . . . open it!" Tameko states.

"I'm coming!" (Tameko doesn't know Paris has been seeing someone, and right now he's in the bedroom taking a shower). *So glad he hasn't heard this whole conversation or else he would have come out of the room acting like he pays rent, and I don't need that shit right now. He's not very friendly. Knowing Tameko, she wouldn't take to his demeanor too well. I haven't had time to tell the girls, and I don't want too, either! Especially Tameko.* Paris thinks. "Anyhoo . . . getting back to your comment—this isn't just an apartment. It's a condo—I don't rent, I own! Remember that!"

"I just thought people who owned . . . own houses, townhouses . . . I never associated apartments with ownership. My bad! I'm just saying. No shade. It all looks the same to me," Tameko yells. "HOLD UP! ARE YOU GOING TO LET ME IN? I CAN'T BELIEVE YOU GOT ME STILL STANDING IN THE FUCKING HALLWAY . . . GRILLING ME . . . JUST BECAUSE YOU GOT A FEW AMENITIES . . . Girl, please! DON'T THINK I AM JEALOUS."

"That sounds like some *hater-ration* SHIT going on," Paris replies.

"You *would* think someone is 'hating on you'—not!" Tameko responds.

*Tameko can't seem to be happy for anybody else except herself. Since we were children, it's always been about Tameko. I can't stand her ass sometimes—so childish.* Paris thinks.

"Getting back to me in this hallway like some hybrid stranger. Girl, bye! Security would've just told me to go upstairs anyway!" Tameko continues, irritated. "He's let me into your apartment/condo before when you weren't even home. We've been friends forever! RIGHT NOW, I AM ABOUT TO END THIS THOUGH. GIRL, YOU TRIPPIN!"

"No, no! No, no!" Paris angrily responds. "He has to call me first and get my permission. This is why I brought this place."

"You still on this. Excuse me! Really? You are going too far. This . . . is some real bullshit," Tameko adds.

"Not at my expense! Not when I pay maintenance fees!" Paris answers.

"What the hell are you rambling on about?" Tameko asked.

"Like I said, no matter what, he'll have to call me and let me know who is coming upstairs. That's one of the benefits of this building. If he can't do his job, I'll have to speak with management."

"You so boogie, Paris," Tameko replies.

"Whatever! I don't have time to be going back and forth with you over something I pay for," Paris responds.

"Honestly, this whole conversation is stupid. Why are you stalling?" Tameko states as Paris finally opens the door. Tameko pushes past Paris. I can't believe you had me in the hallway the entire time.

"I needed to teach your ass a lesson about just walking up to my home without an invite," Paris states.

"Paris, I should be offended, but I am going to ignore your ass . . . because you must be going through something to do some shit like that to me."

"I really don't care. As a matter of fact, why don't you just turn your behind around and go back home?" Paris says, seeing Tameko standing there. "I should've just let your ass stay out in the hallway.

"Try that shit again . . . and see if our friendship doesn't come to an abrupt, end! Girl . . . you being extra right now . . . what's up with you? You better start talking, or I might just leave you ass standing right here, and I will never come back. Why are you talking to me like this, Paris? The only time when women act like this, is either their period is on, or they are getting some dick! Which one is it?"

"Is that the best you can come up with?" Paris adds.

"I am serious right now! You just made me stand out in the hallway like some stranger you didn't know. I felt disrespected. I need some answers fast."

"I'm sorry. I . . .

"It better be the latter, Paris, 'cause that's the only way I am going to let this shit slide. Seriously! Let me be direct. You better be gettin' some DICK. Say something!"

"I . . ." Paris murmurs.

"If you are getting some *L-D, he'd better be putting that shit down hard, and if not, drop his ass . . . because your ass is angry, mean, and bitter. You only get one opportunity to lash out on me like that, and I mean once! You just used yours. Believe that!"* Tameko states.

"You're right! And I am sorry! Please forgive me, Tam."

"Just like that, you want to be forgiven. Give me a minute. Okay, I forgive you," Tameko says, laughing out loud. "Seriously, don't keep me hanging. Are you getting some dick/pole action or what? 'Cause you angry as hell," Tameko asks.

"I am not going to justify that with an answer," Paris replies.

"Biatch, *you better justify something. You just had me standing outside your door like some stranger in the night. I am sorry, but you need to say something.*"

"I said I'm sorry," Paris answers.

"Finally! It's freezing out there. What took you so long to come to the door anyway?" Tameko asks as she blows on her hands, warming them up. "I hate New York weather—sometimes. It's hella cold out there! By the way, where're your clothes, Paris? I don't want to see your personals. If I didn't know you any better, somebody must be up in here. If so, he better be tearing that backside *out!*" she says, laughing loudly. (Tameko is laughing to hide that her feelings were hurt.) "Why else would she not want to let me in?"

"Excuse me but *I am in my house . . . why are you here?*" Paris is getting annoyed.

"Hey . . . Hey . . . Hey . . . did I not just forgive your ass? What's with the attitude? Paris . . . you're acting *real* shady right now. Since when did I have to give you a reason to come over here? I never had to before. Is everything okay? Now, before I turn my ass back around and permanently leave your home, your life . . . I meant what I said. You get just one! You better start talking. What's with you, lately?" Tameko says, her voice rising.

"I'm sorry, girl . . . . just a little stressed," Paris begins.

"Umm . . . why are you stressed? Shit, you must be talking to me all crazy. Seriously, I am about to dead your ass. Our friendship is about to be over, for real. I came over here for some girl talk, wine, and of course, something to eat. Your treating me like some second- class citizen. I...

But now, I don't know if I came to the right person's house. You always got some food." Tameko walks toward the refrigerator and opens it, surprised. *"Where is your food . . . why is your refrigerator so empty?" Now, I know something is up.*

"I'm sorry, I know. I haven't been shopping lately." *I can't seem to keep any food with Leon ass, sitting around all day, eating it all up,* Paris thinks.

"Lately? Girl, the way you like to snack, drink wine, *and* I hardly saw food, a snack or nothing, and since when do you drink beer? I see some bottles in the frig."

"Shit . . . sorry, girl." (Paris forgot there was beer still left in the refrigerator.) "A lot has been going on lately. I was about to go shopping today. I've just been busy. And honestly, if I had known you were coming over, I would have been more prepared."

"More prepared. You always got food. Remember, you used to always say, *'When I grow up, my refrigerator will be stocked, and I will never be hungry again.'"*

"Yeah, well, long way from when we were kids. Shit change."

"What?" Tameko asks.

"Tam, I'm in no mood for girl talk. Do you mind if we . . ." Paris says.

"Hell yeah, now I know something is wrong. You always got time for gossip and girl talk. I haven't seen you in a couple of days, and lately—when I call . . . it goes straight to voicemail," Tameko states.

"Girl talk? Girl, we could have done that over the phone . . . really Tameko!" Paris adds.

"Again, if you had pick up the phone," Tameko responds.

"I just been kind of busy lately. But I'm glad you're back. Come here, let a sister look at you," she says as she hugs her friend. "How was the trip?"

"Besides, when have I ever needed a reason to come to your house, Paris?" *Is there a problem, or is there someone in the picture?* Tameko thinks as she walks over to hang up her coat. "You're acting really strange lately. I thought I heard someone in the bedroom. And why are you in your booty shorts, anyway? You, the type who wears sweatpants and T-shirts?"

"Girl . . . bye! Ah . . . I wasn't expecting anybody, and I damn sure wasn't expecting you," Paris responds. "Besides, you've seen me in booty shorts before."

"Not those! They damn near up your tale. Spare me the visual." Tameko laughs.

"I thought you were still out of town." Paris states, changing the subject. Paris is beginning to feel anxious. *I know he must be out of the shower by now.* Not to mention Tameko knows her all too well.

"I was, but I came back early," Tameko answers vaguely. "The real estate deal fell through, and I decided to come back earlier than I'd expected if that's okay with you. What's with the fourth degree?"

"I'm sorry, don't mind me," Paris answers.

"Well . . . if you must know, I was bored at home, and I decided to come over here to see you. Something tells me you're busy. Paris, you are acting really funny towards me, and I am not used to you talking to me this way. I mean, we joke and all, but you took this shit to a whole new level today," Tameko replies.

"I don't know what else to say, except I am sorry for being so rude," Paris responds.

"Okay. There has never been a problem with me stopping by before without calling. Unless you have someone here for the third or fourth time me asking?" She looks around and then toward the bedroom again. "I noticed your bedroom door closed. Is there someone in there?" Tameko started walking toward the bedroom.

"Ah, excuse me? No!" Paris answers, slightly embarrassed but mostly annoyed. "I'm just surprised to see you. You're right, I do get a little charged. Well . . . since your ass forced yourself in my house, there is some stuff I needed to tell you, but before we get into it, let me get you another glass of wine and refill mine too. In the meantime, let me leave you with this poem. It's called 'Girl Talk'!"

# GIRL TALK

It is just the small things we talk about
The mere conversations we can have at any given moment.
How we can strike up words at a bus stop and never have
known your name. It is just the way we are, it's our
identity. We are so emotional and yet unpredictable at
most. The essence of being can sometimes make us forget
the essence of our sisterhood. The importance of
friendship, closeness we share in a moment or a lifetime
challenges us to leave, come back, or sometimes never at all.
It is the way our hair scrawls up our back when something is wrong.
It is the way our intuition tells us to back off or that something
is not right. Our emotions guide and lead us without notice.
It is that girl talk we love . . . over a bottle
of wine or just because we can.
Girl talk, one of the most important conversations
women can have in a mere second, minutes, or hours
that could last for a lifetime or not at all.

# UNKNOWINGLY, HAPPENED

"Why do I feel like we're not alone?" She walks toward the bedroom. "Do you have company? Is there someone here? Something unknowingly is going on."

"Yes, about that. Let's sit down for a glass of wine. I have something to tell you."

"I don't like the tone of your voice, Paris. What's up?"

"Before we get into it, let me let you read this poem. I know, I usually give them to y'all at the end, but it suits our conversation."

"Ah, Paris, what is going on, seriously?" Tameko states.

"Just read this poem while I pour us a glass of wine. It's called 'Unknowingly Happened.' I hope you enjoy it."

## Unknowingly Happened

I unknowingly let you into my life, my home, and now my bed
I should have taken the time to get to know you, and it has cost me dearly
I let you take me and do what you want, and I should have questioned you. It unknowingly happened, here we are, and it's hard to change back time, staying in this place where my mind is cluttered, and my heart is hurt, it's not where I want to be. I am challenged by my own way of thinking because I know better, and I don't know what has gotten me here.

I cannot seem to get away, and I so desperately want to
be in a better place where love finds me. This is not a
place I thought I would be, I cannot seem to get away. It
unknowingly happened, allowed you in my mind, and it
challenges my thoughts because I can do better.

This space where I am is clouded by the images of pain and
less pleasure. I did not take the time to know who you are,
and it unknowingly happened, showed up in my head, my
life, my home, and now my bed. I can't and I don't want to,
but I do not know how to let you go when you unknowingly
happened to me.

"Paris, this poem, it's not like the rest of them. Is there something
you want to tell me? Do I need to call my peoples or something?
You know me, I was about to get into to my joke bag about how
masturbation is a girl's best friend, but now? But now, are you okay?"
Tameko was puzzled and it showed on her face.

"But now what?" Paris quickly realized she wasn't ready to get into
the details. Paris wearingly smiles.

"I am going to ask you again, what was that about? 'Unknowingly
happened,' what was that about? What have you been up too in these
past couple of days? Or should I say weeks? I've noticed our conversations
have diminished. We didn't get a chance to talk before I left. And now
this poem? Why are you so fidgety?" Tameko states.

"You know me. There is nothing going on at all, girl!" Paris says
as she walks across the room, thinking, *I can see the snide comments
beginning to form inside Tameko's mind. She cannot wait five minutes
before she starts making jokes. Tameko does not like to admit it, but she
is the only hoe in the group. Always has been and always will be. Always
having a comment about someone else's sex life or the lack thereof but never
wanting to discuss her issues. Masturbation, my ass! Tameko is always
between somebody's legs, and it does not matter if he has a title, wife, boo,
or significant other!* "I'm sorry, what were you saying, and by the way,
what happened to Tom, Dick, and Harry, Tameko?"

"Oh, I see, that's your way of changing the subject, trying to throw shade my way. Um . . . I don't know what you mean," Tameko answers.

"Yeah, okay," Paris replies.

"You know what they say, if you're pointing one finger, then three are pointing back at you. So let's not play the judgment games, shall we? Because I know about all your skeletons too. Stop deflecting. What's up, Paris?"

"Tameko? You can't wait five minutes before you start in with your opinions about my life, my sex life, you are too damn nosey and need a life of your own," Paris murmurs.

"*Well, we can't all be like Ms. Perfect Paris,*" Tameko says as she knowingly sizes up her friend. "I don't know if you're aware of the walls you've built around yourself ever since 'Mr. Man' went away and, of course, Joh, too."

"And why is that any of your damn business? You stated it correctly—they were *my* men, Tameko! Not yours!" Paris responds.

"Paris?" Tameko says, switching her tone. "I am extremely worried about you. Again, this poem. What aren't you telling me?"

"Nothing, now you worried about me. Sounds to me like you are just passing judgment as usual. You need to get a life of your own and stay out of other people's business."

"Touché, biatch. Whatever! All you do is 'work, work out, and whatever else boring thing you like to do. Don't get me wrong . . . I do enjoy poetry, though."

"*Why . . . thank you!*" Paris responds.

"Dang, girl, you're starting to become a borderline bore!" Tameko states.

"*Well, before you began interjecting yourself all up into my personal life. I like my 'life' just the way it is. Besides, I have peace of mind and a black book to refer to.*"

"And who's in it, 'Mr. Perfect Paris'?" Tameko says with a laugh. "You got a black book? Stop joking! What black book, Paris? Your 'would've, could've, should've'?"

"Whatever!" Paris is getting really pissed right now. She raises her eyes to let Tameko know to *back* off. "Enough is enough," she continues.

"I've just about had enough of your insulting ass. If you don't shut up . . . I'm going to throw your ass out of my house!"

"I'm sorry, Paris. I didn't realize you were serious." Tameko laughs.

"Speaking, about the 'black books' . . . where yours and who's in it? Where is *your* Mr. Right, or Somebody Else's Man, or should I say . . . Mr. Right-Now Man! 'Cause we both know how you give it up, Tameko." Paris laughs.

"Touché, biatch, again!"

"Do you mind if we change the subject?" Paris says. "I do have something I want to talk to you about."

*Of course, you do!* Tameko thinks. "What?"

"I'm just going to get right to it. Well, the reason why I haven't been participating in our girl talks or sister circle lately is because . . . *I have been seeing someone.*"

"Seriously! What? You have?" Tameko looked surprised. *"WHEN?"*

"Close your mouth, Tameko! Yes, I have!" Paris states.

"Ha ha ha . . . is he still around? When can I meet him? How did you meet? I want all the details. So that is why your ass has been missing in action. You have been wrapped around someone's dick. Girl, I am so happy for you." Tameko laughs aloud.

Paris laughs. "You so crazy. It hasn't been that long."

"Ah . . . yeah, try a couple of months," Tameko states.

"Dating is hard. Have you seen what's walking around out here lately? He's either married, got a girlfriend, or a situation."

"I know what you mean. Men don't want to date, and some ladies are making it hard for a lady to meet a real man."

"I'm sorry, I don't share dick or money with no one. Especially another woman. Oh, I'm sorry, Tameko, no point intended." Paris chuckles.

"You got jokes. Touché again, biatch. I heard that! Now, getting back to Mr. Perfect Paris . . ." Tameko laughs.

Paris goes on to state, "Not to mention the unavailable, unemotional man who doesn't have time or emotions to give, and then there is the brushing off a man, build-him-up man, clean-his-ass-up man anymore! I am done."

"Girl, I been there too, and I get it."

"That shit is annoying." Paris's voice rises.

"You get so fired up. Paris, relax." Tameko laughs.

"I'm trying, but this one unknowingly happened, it was unexpected, and it came out of nowhere. After so much disappointment, I just felt lonely, and there he was."

"I understand. We've all experienced that before."

"Don't you dare make a joke. I see it in your face, Tameko."

"I wasn't, okay, maybe I was, but then, I wanted to be in the moment with you. I said to myself, 'Tameko, don't do it.'" Tameko chuckles.

"Whatever, I hate talking to you sometimes. I am about to get another glass of wine. We about to get into some heavy shit!" Paris adds.

"Bring the bottle. I might need a refill. Do you at least got some crackers?"

# ASSIMILATE

"So . . . . where were we? You said something about me being lonely, but the truth is—I'm never lonely or alone. There's a difference. Which one are you, Tameko?"

Tameko turns around out of concern. "I thought I heard someone in the bedroom, again. Paris, is there someone here? I know I'm not just hearing things.

Yes! About that? I . . ."

"Hi . . . babe, you didn't tell me we had company."

"We! What is he saying?" Tameko responds.

Paris mutters, "I wasn't going too."

"Hi there!" Leon says again as he walks out of the bedroom and toward Tameko.

Tameko swings around in surprise. "And who are you?"

"I'm Leon. Paris's man. She didn't tell you?"

Tameko gasped at the sight of Leon. She was in total surprise when she saw him walk out of the room. *What the hell*, Paris, what?"

*"I'm sorry, where are my manners? You must be Tameko. I recognized you from your picture. You are a beautiful lady."*

*"Thank you, and who are you?"* Tameko said, noticeably taken *aback*. She had no idea Paris was seeing someone, much less walking out of her bedroom as if he lived there. *When did this happen?* Tameko thought. *I am Tameko! Paris's best friend!*

"Well, it's nice to meet you finally, Tameko! Paris talks about you and the girls all the time. I think it's a sister circle, sisterhood—it's four of you ladies . . . some shit like that."

"Excuse me!" Tameko states.

*"Excuse my directness. I wasn't trying to be rude. I was stating the obvious."* Leon notices Tameko's attitude.

"Getting back to my girl. It's about damn time!" Tameko exclaims. "When were you going to tell me or any of us for that matter?"

"I was going to, but—"

"Hi, let's start again. My name is Leon." Leon extends his hand.

"Leon who?" Tameko walks to the other side of the room.

"As stated, I am Paris's man! If you didn't know. We weren't expecting you, or anyone for that matter."

"We? You are very sarcastic . . . " Tameko chimes in.

Paris began, "I'm sorry, Tameko. I was going to catch up with you when you came back, but you showed up earlier than I expected."

*"Hey, hey, hey!* Why are you checking my girl like she's your daughter? She *is* a grown woman, which means she doesn't have to explain anything to you if she doesn't want to," Leon chimes in.

"So . . . what are you, her bodyguard, now?" Tameko answers.

*"Stop it guys . . . this is getting out of hand.* Tameko, I didn't have time to talk to you or the girls. This is happening all so fast."

"What do you mean it all happened so fast? What are you doing in Paris's house like you're paying the mortgage?"

Paris mutters, *"That will be the day.* She's just a little surprised, Leon."

"I get it, she needs to understand that, baby, but ah, she needs to lower her tone . . . in my house."

*"Who, me? I'm standing right here, Mr. Man.* Paris, so you're lying now?" Tameko says, turning back around to Paris. "I just asked you if someone was here!"

"This . . . umm . . . this is Leon . . . Leon Baker," Paris responds.

"I heard that part. I'm sorry, no disrespect, but *he* ain't even your type! You—slipping! You're telling me you're seeing this dude?"

"Yes!" Paris responds.

"Wait a minute! I am standing right here, and I can hear you," Leon responds.

"Like I give a damn. How long and how did you meet this . . . ?" Tameko replies.

"We met at the local market down on Fourth Ave. Umm . . . do you both want some wine? *How's a glass of red? I suddenly feel like I need some.*" Paris races to pour the wine as she rubs the back of her neck while feeling stressed.

"No! I don't need no damn wine," Tameko responds. "*I want to know who is this man, and what is he doing here? Looking like he's every bit of what needs to still grow up. Seriously!*"

"Excuse me, I've listened to your ass long enough. Paris doesn't have to explain anything to you. I'm her man, and this conversation has gone on long enough. My name is Leon. I am Paris's man! We've been seeing each other for a while now."

"What, a while now, when? Where did you say you met him?" Tameko asks.

"At the grocery store down on Fourth, really, Tameko . . . Why do you ask?"

"I don't care. Really, I don't. You need to take his ass back down on Fourth Ave. and leave him there. He is all wrong for you—no need to drag this on."

"Well, since you must know, um . . . Tanya . . . " Leon interrupts.

"It's Tameko, smartass. You heard me the first time. Tameko!"

"As I was saying, Tameko! We just started talking and realized we liked a lot of the same things: playing pool, going to see live poetry readings, dancing, and of course hot-ass sex. I understand you don't have a man. Whoops . . . yeah!"

"Excuse me, Paris . . . you telling this man my business?"

I'm . . . sorry, Tameko!"

"Can I speak with my friend . . . or do I need to get your permission first? And—I need to speak to my friend alone. Do you mind?"

"Umm . . . sure . . . no problem," Leon responds. "Baby, I'm going to the store and get that orange juice you wanted. I'll be right back."

"Okay, babe," Paris answers.

"Girl, you've assimilated into his mess," Tameko faintly states.

*This "chick" is gonna have me say something,* Leon thinks as he walks out of the house. *I don't take lightly to NO woman disrespecting me, period!*

"Did you say something? Babe?" Paris yells from across the room.

"Naw—I am good," Leon responds as he walks out the door.

# ASSIMILATE

*I wanted to assimilate into being the person you wanted
me to be, so that you love me. I think about all the
things you did and how I let you do them,
Just to assimilate into your power of love, it hurt so bad.
I realized you're not going to change, and the unfortunate value of you
doesn't work for me.
I wish I knew how to say goodbye without feeling guilty
A constant inclination of how I love, it's hard for you to understand.
I love by the feeling you give, but now I know it wasn't real.
It was just a false assimilation of who really you are.
You sent your representative, and I looked past him. I would have given
you        anything of me. Love isn't supposed to feel this way to me, I
guess I must      learn to look within. A fool waist for it to choose them
and not let it create false identity within. We are masked by our feelings
of emotions, and it covers who we really are. I imagine love and the
capacity of where it will take me. I tried to assimilate into being someone
other than what this will be with you, a false assimilation of love.*

# ABUSE TO MY SOUL

Tameko starts, "PARIS, WHAT IS GOING ON HERE? AND WHY DIDN'T YOU TELL ME?"

"I don't know. You know how it is . . . when you meet someone . . . just want to keep it a secret for a while. This time, maybe it will work out."

"I guess. I can understand that," Tameko responds.

"But shit . . . this—this is getting heavy. He started changing," Paris states.

"Changing how? I can see that. THIS DUDE IS CONTROLLING, ABUSIVE, NOT TO MENTION RUDE, AND VERY DISRESPECTFUL. I just met him, and I don't like him for you," Tameko says.

"Honestly, I don't think I like him either," Paris answers.

"Then why don't you ask him to leave?" Tameko asks.

Paris says more calmly, "It was good in the beginning, and I liked having him around. But—"

"But . . . what? Don't take this the wrong way . . . something is off with this guy," Tameko states.

"Lately, *I don't know*. He is not the kind of guy I hoped him to be," Paris responds.

"What do you mean?"

"Once I got to know him and the newness wore off . . . " Paris walks across the room nervously.

"What are you trying to say?" Tameko demands.

Paris wanted to come right out, but it was difficult to admit the truth. "Well, it happened so fast. This tall, gorgeous brother came a-calling. It had been *so* long. By the time Leon came to my rescue, I was damn near 'cummin' in my pants. At that point, I didn't care. I just wanted to be held. I wanted to feel like I mattered to someone. He was what I thought I needed him to be and wanted. Honestly, I let my emotions get the best of me. I admit I should've taken more time. I should've gotten to know him better! His outer appearance did not match up to his inner being. At first, I thought I liked it, someone taking control and handling things. But I guess I lost myself in the interim." Paris begins to think, *How do you tell your closest friends, the ones who come to you for advice . . . you're no longer following your own?*

"I don't follow. What are you trying to say?" Tameko asks.

"I let him move in three weeks later," Paris responds.

"YOU DID WHAT? He moved into your house, and why would you do a thing like that?"

"Honestly, loneliness! Plus, he sent his representative, talked a good game, and the sex well—communicated well."

"Well, did he at least have a job, credit, and benefits?"

"Too soon, Tameko," Paris adds.

"I tried." Tameko chuckles.

"Honestly, it all happened so fast I wasn't sure what he had," Paris admits, "and I don't think I cared at that moment. I was tired of being alone. I just never thought . . ."

"You just never thought what?"

"I don't know what I thought. It turned out to be a bad decision," Paris responds.

"If it makes you feel any better, Paris, it has happened to all of us. What did he say that MADE you want to let this man into your house? Or should I say, what did he bring to the table? This is not like you!"

"He had some good qualities. There were some yeses and nos," Paris states.

"Yeses and nos? Well, what were the yeses and the nos?"

"Yes, he does work construction. He said he had all his papers in order," Paris adds.

"Papers in order? You mean he was looking for a green card marriage? I can't!" Tameko laughs.

"No! Meaning, he was in the union and he would always have consistent work. But I . . . "

"Which meant his work life was iffy? Did he at least come in with the first month's rent and some groceries, as you would tell us to do?"

"I at least stated that from the jump. Leon didn't come in empty-handed. As per Steve Harvey . . . I had requirements! He had a month's rent and brought some stuff," Paris states.

"Did you?" Tameko laughs.

And now I find out—he doesn't have good credit, no real papers and the "French benefits" aren't that great, either—if you know what I mean!"

"NO, I don't know what you mean by French benefits. Please explain."

"Girl . . . you know what I mean. I don't have to spell out every damn detail."

"OH . . . You *mean* he isn't nine inches long and three inches wide? No golf pole to slide down on?" Tameko responds.

"Not at all," Paris responds. "I have to admit. I was horny, and I buckled. But damn . . . this is all wrong."

Laughing, Tameko replies, "I have been there too, girl. No judgment. Just because they're tall and have long fingers doesn't necessarily mean they're hanging."

"Well . . . I guess one out of three isn't bad. And then there's . . . there's the finger-licking good."

"Oh, you mean, since he wasn't hanging, he at least needed to know how to clear the plate," Tameko says with a laugh.

"To be honest," Paris says, "he did manage to get that right. But— I'm the kind of woman who needs a golf pole every once in a while."

"Girllll. I know what you mean." Tameko chuckles.

"Absolutely!" Paris smirks. "Can we get back to me . . . Tameko? I don't need your sarcasm right now. This is hard enough telling you this mess."

"I'm sorry . . . go ahead."

"I think he's becoming some type of squatter in my house. He won't leave, and I can't get him out, but that's not the worst of it. I went to housing court and inquired about squatter's rights, and they informed me, if he can prove residency that he has been living with me for more than 30 days, I will have to evict him out of *my* house. Who knew? It seemed like he knew what to do, and I didn't even have a clue. He got into my house, he started having his mail come here. I open my mailbox and there it was. He didn't even ask for permission. Can you believe that shit?" Paris's voice heightens. "I NEVER TOLD HIM TO DO THAT."

"Really? WHAT! FORWARD HIS MAIL?" Tameko yells back.

"Yes, I'm done. You can't even know how much I want this man out of my house," Paris states.

"Wow. I am sorry. Is there anything I can do?"

"I didn't know how to tell you this but wait—there is more."

"What . . . there's more! I think I need another glass of wine." Tameko walks toward the kitchen table to pour another glass.

Paris begins to pace back and forth. "I don't know I—he's becoming aggressive toward me."

"Why are you whispering in your own house?"

Paris ignores Tameko's comment. She continues, "I mean, at first, it was just the small things like name-calling, cussing at me, but now . . . "

"Now what?" Tameko inquires.

"It's happening all the time now. The name-calling has gotten worse. Calling me names like *BIATCH, STUPID,* and *FAT.*" Paris pauses, looking at Tameko. "Do I look fat?"

"Hell naw! Hell . . . I'm jealous of that body!"

"He caught me off guard," Paris says as she continues her pacing. "I didn't see it coming. It was the small comments like 'Be quiet,' 'Take off that make-up, go take that off,' 'You shouldn't wear that,' 'I'm not finished talking to you, come here!' At first, I tried to ignore it and even laughed it off," Paris recalls.

"I'm sorry, but do I hear you right?" Tameko begins to pace back and forth. "Are you telling me this man is putting his hands on you?"

"He has been pushing me a lot more lately. Girl"—Paris hesitates—"I thought that would be the end of it. But then, he started the light pushing, and later, it became harder. I tried telling him to stop."

But I—"

"Excuse me, you are kidding me, right? Pushing you? It's time to call my family. We don't play that shit. When did you notice it was getting out of hand? Oh my god, Paris, I've known you a long time. I'm sorry. I knew something was wrong. I just never thought it was this."

"You think *I* thought this would happen to me, Tameko?"

"No! I don't mean. I'm not judging. I just meant—"

"I know you not. I'm sorry for getting upset with you. Honestly, this is not what I pictured for me. I am scared all the time. When the pushing became hitting, I knew I had to do something. I knew it had gone on too long," Paris states.

Tameko was almost in tears, but she didn't want Paris to see her . . . so she walked off toward the kitchen to refill her glass again.

"You know what, I'mma be drunk before I leave your house. This shit is crazy."

"When he hit me on my back, that's one thing, but when he slapped me in my face, it left a bruise, and I had to cover it up so no one would notice." Paris's eyes were beginning to water up.

"I'm so sorry," Tameko whispers. "I'm shocked by all this."

As Paris continues to speak, she feels her mouth getting dry. "Hey, give me a minute. I need some water." She walks into the kitchen, thinking it's good to tell someone. *At first, I thought I like what I had met. His position, his stance, his manhood until he turned it on me. I hate to admit it, but once again, I made another bad choice. Here I am always giving advice, but my own advice betrayed me, and I stopped listening.*

"Are you all right, Paris?" Tameko yells.

Paris talks to herself while in the kitchen. *I thought I looked good, but when Leon came along, I began to think something was wrong with me, or at least that was how he made me feel. I can't seem to get a man, much less keep one. Being single, who wants to admit to their friends, they're still on the waiting list? Another failed relationship!*

*It's only now I'm beginning to see the types of relationships I've been attracted too. Like Iyanla says, when you're born out of toxicity . . . you're bound to continue in toxicity."*

"Paris, are you good? You need some help?" Tameko yells.

Paris responds, "I'm good. I'll be right there." She continues to think to herself. *I'm surprised to be here. It feels like it's my fault—the signs were there, but I ignored them. I counsel women about abuse all the time. Now, I'm the abusee. How did I get here?*

"ARE YOU GOOD? Why didn't you tell someone?" Tameko asks.

"I don't know. Honestly, that's why I couldn't go to the movies last month with you and the girls. I had a black eye. I couldn't let you and the girls see me that way. I feel like I just keep apologizing for that punk-ass nigga."

Tameko notices Paris walking toward her and reaches out to hug her. "Hey, you good? Is there anything I can do?"

"I'm sorry."

"You're sorry? You don't need to be embarrassed about anything. This happens more than you know."

"How do you think I feel? I'm completely embarrassed! Sometimes, the loneliness gets louder than the words. I could no longer hear myself think. I missed the touch, the presence, and the comfort of a man. I can't remember the last time I—but he's breaking my spirit. I then realized my peace of mind was going away, and I needed to do something. It will overtake you," Paris says.

"Damn, girl," Tameko responds. "How long it's been?"

"Long enough to know it doesn't matter how long. *No one* has the right to abuse, hurt, or make you feel less than. And when the quietness becomes too loud, well, it's time to find something else to do. Hobbies are important!"

"Shit, where is he? I need to whip his ass. I'm horny *for* you, Paris. Even if you don't think I understand, I do."

"Leave it to you to always find humor," Paris says with a weak laugh.

"I'm just saying: I could find you someone if it was that serious," Tameko replies.

"No. The last time you did that . . . well, let's just say you're not allowed to fix me up with anyone else again." Paris laughs.

"Looks like I'm going to have to keep looking out for my sister," Tameko says.

"If there's one thing I always tell women I counsel," Paris says, "it's that when there is abuse, there is no love. Love has no pain. It's patient and giving. It's nurturing, understanding, it respects you. You matter. I forgot about this!"

"You need to remember this next time because they will take what they want from you and leave you with nothing, sucking up all your nutrients. Paris, baby," Tameko states.

***

"I think I hear him. Let's just change the subject. I don't want him to think we were talking about him."

"You don't want him to think, so what if we were? It looks like Mr. Meatball is back," Tameko jokingly states, hearing footsteps on the stairs. "Paris, does he have a key to your place?" Tameko asks.

"Yes, I gave him one when he moved in."

"You did what? But you just met, dang, wonder why he so comfortable. You gave him carte blanche. It took me a minute to get my key. See what DICK will do to a biatch. Drive us completely crazy." Tameko squeals.

***

"Hey, baby!" she says as Leon walks through the door.

"Okay. I see you're still here. I thought I made it clear: you needed to leave, Tanya."

"It is Tameko. Jack . . ."

"Tam. Whatever your name is."

"Excuse me! Wait a minute . . . brother . . . you got the right one now!" Tameko answers.

"Paris, why is this woman still here?" Leon's voice rises. "I thought she would have left behind me. You know I don't allow company in the house when I'm not here!"

"I can explain . . . " Paris says.

"Why am *I* still here? And why does she need to explain in her own damn house? Are you serious? What did you even say your name was again?"

"Leon! My name is Leon Baker. Paris's man. This . . . is my house."

"Not for long, man! And *I am* Paris's best friend."

Leon grabs Paris's arm. "Paris, what is she talking about? Should we talk in private? Can I see you in the bedroom? Now!"

Paris shrugs him away. "Whatever you have to say to me, you can say in front of her. We tell each other everything."

"Everything?" Leon replies.

"Yes, everything, Leon!"

"You know what she is talking about. The cat is out of the bag," Tameko interjects. "We do not have secrets between us."

"Tameko, maybe you should leave," Paris says suddenly.

"LEAVE!" Tameko responds. "YOU'RE ASKING ME TO LEAVE OVER THIS TWO-BIT OF A HUSTLER. HE'S THE ONE WHO SHOULD BE LEAVING!"

"I don't know you," Leon interjects, "but if my woman asks you to leave, then maybe you should."

"*YOUR WOMAN*!" Tameko yells. "*YOUR WOMAN*! If she were *YOUR WOMAN*, you wouldn't be putting your hands on her. If she were *YOUR WOMAN*, you wouldn't be disrespecting her. A real man never puts his hands on his woman, Mr. Man! *YOUR WOMAN*! Give me a break! You wouldn't know a real woman because you're not a real man. You're just a momentary mishap! Do not get it twisted."

"WHAT THE HELL . . . is she talking about, Paris?" Leon yells. "YOU'RE TELLING OUR BUSINESS? I don't want people in our business! And I told you that before, and I don't want people here when I'm not home."

"I know, baby," Paris answers in a shaky voice. "She was just concerned, and I let her understand some things." Paris had known that Leon would be mad about Tameko being here. *Ever since he moved in, he has acted as if no one can come here, and I'm not allowed to have any company in my house.*

"Wait! Am I REALLY hearing this man tell MY GIRL THAT THIS IS HIS HOUSE AND SHE CAN'T HAVE COMPANY IN HER OWN HOUSE?" Tameko yells. "No, this isn't what I am hearing at all. The home she bought on her own. No . . . this—"

"Wait—Tameko!" Paris says.

"NO! I have known you for over 15 years and this sideway walking sorry excuse for a man . . . he is talking to you like a child, is he crazy!"

Leon starts yelling again. "UNDERSTAND THIS! I PAY THE BILLS AROUND HERE . . . THIS IS MY HOUSE! AND IF I ASKED YOU TO LEAVE . . . YOU'VE GOT TO GO. YOU GOT TWO MINUTES TO GET OUT OF MY HOUSE!"

"I AM ABOUT TO JUMP ON HIS ASS. MAYBE I SHOULD CALL MY GIRLS. SO WE CAN BEAT—PARIS, ARE YOU HEARING THIS?" Tameko responds. "HAS HE CUT OUT YOUR DAMN TONGUE OR SOMETHING?"

Paris seems scared but then states, "You know what . . . you're right, Tameko." Paris suddenly feels confident to speak up. As if she was waking up from a bad dream. "Wait a minute," she says as she turns around to face Leon. "THIS IS MY HOUSE, Leon!"

"Excuse me? I know you are not raising your voice to me," Leon responds.

"WHAT BILLS DO YOU PAY?" PARIS THUNDERS. "THE CABLE AND CON EDISON? ONLY SO YOU CAN SIT AROUND WATCHING WRESTLING AND EATING ALL MY FOOD, ALL DAY? YOU TELL ME YOU'RE WORKING, BUT THEN I FIND OUT AFTER YOU MOVED IN THAT YOU DON'T HAVE A JOB! EVERY DAY YOU'RE SUPPOSEDLY GETTING UP . . . GETTING DRESSED . . . GOING TO WORK . . . BUT INSTEAD, YOU'RE GOING TO THE POOL HALL!"

"Girl, you do know who you're talking too. I don't take kindly to no woman speaking to me like this," Leon interjects. "I am going to ask you to be quiet before I embarrass you in front of your friend."

"You already did that. I am embarrassed for myself. I don't let men talk to me this and not from a bum like you!"

"Bum! Girl, you really asking for it." Leon's anger rises.

"REALLY! LEON, YOU HAVE NOTHING TO OFFER A GOOD WOMAN BECAUSE YOU DON'T HAVE ANYTHING TO OFFER YOURSELF. YOU'RE AN OPPORTUNIST . . . . LIVING OFF OTHER PEOPLE'S LABOR. Oh, and those papers you were supposed to have? They were FALSE! Oh, yeah, I checked! Oh, you thought I didn't know! Yes. You're not in no damn union! For the record, I PAY ALL THE BILLS, BUY THE FOOD, and TAKE CARE OF YOUR NEEDS. ME!"

"Oh, hell, no!" Tameko adds. "You got to go, brother! Cause NOW—you are cutting in on my ends!"

Paris feels her pressure beginning to rise. "I can't anymore, Leon!"

"WOMAN, YOU TRYING TO SHOW ME UP IN FRONT OF YOUR FRIEND HERE?" Leon answers. "You know I oughta—" He raises his hand.

"You oughta what?" Paris responds.

"I . . . girl your making me MAD. And you know what happens when Daddy gets mad. I—"

Paris stands closer to Tameko. "I do know! I know all too well! I should have never allowed you to talk to me in such a manner. The first time you cursed, pushed me, I should have never let you get away with it. It went too far. I admit I was in denial about how much you were hurting me. . ."

"Like I said . . . DID YOU FORGET WHO I AM? YOU TRYING TO PLAY ME, AND YOU KNOW I DON'T LIKE THAT."

"THE PROBLEM IS YOU FORGOT WHO *I* AM. I'M YOUR WOMAN, AND YOU SUPPOSED TO BE MY MAN. MY PROVIDER, MY PROTECTOR, MY PLEASER! But all I ever got from you from the time you moved in was—grief! And ungratefulness! I'm trying to help you. Brush you off! You were supposed to be my restorer, but all you came to do was steal, kill, and destroy me." Paris begins to walk across the room.

"DON'T WALK AWAY FROM ME, WOMAN!" Leon yells.
"WE'RE NOT DONE UNTIL I SAY WE'RE DONE! I AM THE
MAN! WE GET DONE WHEN I SAY SO!"

"He done lost his mind. Is this man crazy?" Tameko says as she
crosses her arms.

"I never thought I'd be here, but I guess you can never say never
because if it happened to me, it could happen to anyone! I saw all the
signs, but I ignored them. I let you disrespect me, put your hands on
me, alienate me from my family and friends . . . and you know what's
worse? You are living in my house. This . . . is MY house!"

"Tell him, Paris!" Tameko cheers.

"Shut UP!" Paris and Leon say in unison.

Tameko steps back.

"What you gonna do without me?" Leon continues. "Before I came,
you had no life. I made you feel *good*. I made you feel like a woman. I
GAVE YOU SUBSTANCE. SEE HOW QUICKLY WE FORGET!"

"YOU GAVE ME SUBSTANCE?" Paris responds. "I THINK
YOU GOT IT TWISTED! I GAVE *YOU* THE MAN CARD. I PUT
YOU ON. I LEVELED YOU UP. I TAUGHT YOU HOW TO SIT
UPRIGHT!"

"YOU MADE . . . ME? Never!"

"OH YES, I DID!" Paris argues back.

"YOU ARE MEANINGLESS!" Leon interjects.

"You right about one thing," Paris continues. "You told me all the
right things—but I already knew those things! I just got lost in my
silence. I forgot who's first. It's me. If I hadn't forgotten my worth, I
wouldn't be here, and I forgot His purpose for me. He wants me to be
happy."

"Did you get that, Mr. Man?" Tameko adds.

"Whatever!" Leon responds.

"I should have done this a long time ago," Paris says as she walks
toward the door. "It's time for you to go, LEON! OH . . . before,
I forget. I went to criminal court today and, ah, I got an order of
protection out on your ass. Yes, I filed a police report. It's all on record.
I showed the judge the pictures I took. Yes, pictures! I knew I would

need some proof. Painfully, I took them myself. I lost faith in me, but now I'm learning how to stand. Today is the day. It's over!"

"Say what? You're throwing me out of my house?" Leon sputters.

"THIS IS MY HOUSE, Leon! YOU WOULDN'T HAVE TO GO IF YOU KNEW HOW TO TREAT A WOMAN, IF YOU KNEW HOW TO BE ACCOUNTABLE AND RESPONSIBLE! THIS . . . COULD HAVE BEEN OUR HOUSE TOGETHER. BUT YOU RUINED THAT."

"TELL HIM, PARIS," Tameko says as she walks toward the closet. "TELL HIM—THIS IS YOUR HOUSE! IF HE WANTS IT, HE CAN GET IT. I AM NOT SCARED." She pulls out a baseball bat and points it at Leon.

"Tanya . . . Tameko or whatever you call yourself . . . . You need to stay your ass over there, or you can both get it, too!"

"PACK YOUR BAGS AND GET OUT! Paris continues. "Don't even think of trying anything. I'm ready for that, too." She reaches into her bag and grabs her mace. You've been an abuse to my soul, and that's not how a man is supposed to love you, treat you. You are abusive!"

"Whatever. I don't want to hear no poetry shit, I'm outta here," Leon says.

"Oh, and Leon," Paris adds, "I know I'm not the first woman you did this to. I spoke to Pam. She was at the courthouse today, reinstating her order of protection."

Leon turns around looking surprised and states, "All right, all right, I guess it's time for me to go, then. I'll be at my momma's house. Paris, baby, you know where to find me. They always come back for the LD."

"The LD? Is that all you have to offer? And you didn't even do that right. I can take care of myself. Bye!" Paris states.

"*Not the way I do it,*" Leon shoots back as he walks out the house.

"Hey, don't worry about your belongings. I'll have them shipped to your MOMMA'S house! *And* she is going to be pissed. You know, she doesn't even want your broke ass there. Goodbye!" Paris closes the door behind Leon.

"*Dang girl, whew . . . that was a lot. I am so glad I was here,*" Tameko says.

*"I am glad you were here too, Tam. Honestly, I couldn't get him to leave, and I didn't have enough strength to keep fighting him. I'm so glad he is gone."* Paris sighs in relief.

"A bum will always find comfort in your space if you allow it. I am proud of you, girl," Tameko says as the women meet at the couch. "I know that wasn't easy."

"It wasn't, but it helped you were here! I needed to admit that fear and embarrassment is why he lasted so long."

"I understand. Do me a favor: call, yell, scream, but don't put yourself through things you don't have to. Do not allow excuse where none are needed. It's not worth it."

Paris shrugs. *"I'll remember. Look who is the poet, now!"* She chuckles.

"You remember why we formed the sister club to be empowering and be supportive of one another," Tameko states.

"I remember," Paris says softly. "I'll be fine." *It's quite easy to love the wrong man, especially when your own insecurities surface. And when the loneliness gets louder than the words, misery will follow,* Paris thinks to herself while Tameko prepares to leave.

"You're right," Tameko answers. "But in the end, it's also important to remember who you are and to love thyself, first. Look, I got to go, girl."

"I will be moving forward," Paris replies.

Tameko says as she checks her phone, "Can you handle things from here? Are you sure Knucklehead isn't coming back?"

"No, he's not that stupid. If he comes back, I'll call the cops. Leon will hit a woman, but he will not hit a man. Besides, he doesn't want to go back to jail. He knows I've got friends on the inside who'll be waiting on his punk ass, and they like men, too!" Paris laughs.

"I know that's right." Tameko chuckles. "All right, girl, let me say good night. This . . . has been quite a night. Hey, before I leave, I can sure use one of those poems. They're always uplifting. Oh, have you spoken to Alanna lately?" Tameko inquires.

"No, why?"

"I think you two should talk."

"I've called her, but she hasn't returned any of my calls. Is there something wrong? How's her sister Jennifer since she came to live with Alanna?"

"I think you should talk with Alanna."

"What's up? I can't wait. I hate surprises. Tam?"

"Don't do that. It's not fair. You only called me when your ass wants the tea. Anyhoo, a lot has been going on. Alanna needs to tell you herself."

"What do you mean a lot has been going on?" Paris asks, concerned.

"You'll have to get it from her. They've been going through it. She is stressed out."

"Really. What is going on? You know I hate being left out of the business."

"Yes, we know. But this isn't about you, Paris, and when you speak with Alanna, just listen. Be supportive and be there for her in the moment."

"What—what are you talking about?"

"Honestly, sometimes you make everything about you when it isn't. I'm just saying. I hope you improved on your listening skills."

*Okay, okay,* Paris thinks, *I've always been a great listener. I have no idea what Tameko is talking about. She's always trying to transfer her nonsense onto me.* "Isn't it time for your ass to go?" Paris states.

"I guess, since you put it that way." *Look who's being aggressive now. You should have been aggressive with that,* Tameko thinks. "Paris, sometimes it's not about you! And on that note—good night!" She turns to leave.

"Thank you for stopping by, Tameko. It was really good seeing you," Paris says as she walks her out. "I am so grateful for you, and I love you."

Tameko turns to look at Paris. "Remember what I told you. Just be a friend and listen. Good night."

"I told you . . . I will!"

"Oh, before I go . . . my poem?"

"I'll text it to you. I think it's better when you can sit down to read it. It's called 'Abuse to My Soul.'"

# ABUSE TO MY SOUL

*Every time you beat me with your words,*
*I felt it as if you struck me with your hand.*
*I never understood the defamation of character,*
*nor the hatred displayed.*
*As if I had just imagined it.*
*Life has a way of telling lost souls the untold truths,*
*And those very same truths may not be what you want to hear.*
*Life has a way of showing us the grass*
*is not always greener on the other side where there are thorns!*
*So, what do we do when the words?*
*And the venom spilled become so crystal clear?*
*When the truth becomes undeniable and unavoidable?*
*It's Hell!*
*Does the abuse have to result in death?*
*Is it a means to an end?*
*I wish I knew how to determine what love is*
*Without being battered or broken.*
*Do the misunderstanding and the fallacy of love*
*Become a dream that most may never feel?*
*Some say "tell," and some say "be quiet."*
*If only life came with a book of answers*
*Instead of experiences.*
*If only we could have learned*
*Where others have failed: never living to tell!*
*Because one can never tell the demons*
*Waiting to be expelled!*

# BAD-BOY SYNDROME

*Could you believe this shit? I have to go back to my momma's house? How dare she throw me out of my own house? I need to talk to someone . . . let me give my boy Brian a call.* Leon thinks.

"Hello?" Brian answers.

"Yeah—ah, this is Leon. Long time no hear from, what good?"

*Good. I know you're not calling me after what you did to my sister. It's good thing I haven't seen your ass.* "What's good and what do you want?"

"Nothing really. Hey, I am sorry about your sister. I just wanted to talk to you. I didn't mean to hurt your sister's feelings, but she was too good for me. I need a little edge if you know what I mean," Leon states.

"No. I don't. All I know is—she really liked you and you played her. So *why* are you calling me?" Brian responds.

"I just need a place to stay for a minute until I can get my stuff together. I really don't want to go back to Mom's house."

"EXCUSE ME? YOU *PLAYED* MY SISTER AND NOW YOU ARE CALLING ME TO HELP YOU AFTER YOUR LADY THREW YOU OUT OF 'YOUR HOUSE'. ARE YOU SERIOUS RIGHT NOW?" Brian raises his voice.

"Yes! Because we're boys no matter what. Remember, when I held you down in the joint and you promised me, you'll always hold me down when I got out," Leon responds.

"Yeah, but that was so long ago, we did a lot of bad-boy stuff back then. I paid you back many times. I don't owe you nothing!"

"Okay, okay—I just need your help. I didn't mean to come at you like that, but I don't have nowhere else to go and I can't go back home."

"Who is this woman anyway? Do I know her?"

"No! I doubt it. We met down on Fourth. It was organically done. Ha ha!"

"Organically. Nigga, you from the streets. Who talks like that? Not you. What happened? I thought you like this woman? What did you do that would cause her to throw your ass out of the house?" Brian asks.

"MAN, ALL THAT IS NOT IMPORTANT. *I'm not going to tell you all our business. Just know it didn't work out, and now I am calling on my boy. You know how we do: love them, handle the situation, made sure they know we are the "man" of the home, nothing more!"*

**"OH, I see . . . so you still on that bad-boy syndrome shit. You still think you're still the man after all these years. Move up in their house, control the situation, get it, take what they have, and then do nothing to maintain it. I'm glad she caught on. My sister didn't, but it's all good. I bet she won't let another nigga hurt her again. I put her onto the game. So miss me with all your bullshit."**

"Yeah, well I just need a place where I can crash for a moment, until I can get my situation together."

"No, you're looking for someone else to play with, lay-up on, continue being that bad boy. The syndrome is over! And no, I can't help you! Go back home to your momma house, her baby boy."

"What you on some poetry shit. Sound like my girl."

"No, brother. I just know how you think. You don't learn, and probably the best place for you is your momma house or jail. It's the only place where you are comfortable."

"Really, you gonna try to play me."

"Play you. I don't have to play you, you played yourself. The person who raised you, taught you nothing except how to get over on people. Hustle women out of what little they have in order to give you what you will not give them. The boy who never grows up to be a man. Like K. Michelle says, 'Can't raise a man when he is still a boy.'"

"You are sounding whipped right now, brother. We used to do this together. Brian, play the games, run games, I'm still good."

"You are not good, and the sad thing is you don't know it."

"I know you not gonna just leave me hanging."

"What we used to do and who I am today is not the same brother you used to know. I'm not your mother, and I'm not your fallback guy either. You are a grown-ass man. Grow up! Goodbye, Leon!"

"Wait . . . whatever. I don't need nobody!"

Brian hangs up.

# BAD-BOY SYNDROME

I am the original bad boy, and I have a syndrome. I
want what I want, and I don't want to work hard for
it, and if I do—I want you to acknowledge it.
I want to be a part of the street conversations even if
it doesn't make sense because when they are talking,
I just can't walk away—just to please you.
I need the streets and the relationships it encompasses even if it makes
you wait a little while longer. You like the aggressive side of who I
am, and sometimes it aggravates me when you don't understand. I am
just a bad boy, caught up in this syndrome of a life I've come to love.
I may want you, but I can't let them see me sweatin' you, or
they may see it as being weak, and I'd rather ignore you just
to maintain my respect. Do not argue with me to understand
who I am, but respect my plight, purpose, and persona. Your
nature is to serve me, and mine is to penetrate you physically,
mentally, and rarely emotionally and sometimes financially.
I need to nullify your thoughts, allowing me to cultivate your
soul, to manipulate your being, by mere spoken words. Even if
I don't mean any of it, you are intrigued by my presence, and
what I falsely represent the essence of who you are. In the end,
knowing I have nothing for you, I still want you to wait for me
until I feel I am ready to be with you in the most simplistic way.
This is who I am: a bad boy for life.

# REASONING

*When I think back to that warm summer night in July 2015,* Paris remembers, *the summer breeze caresses my mind, body, and soul. I find myself slipping into a melodic mood of making love, and I want to feel the touch of a man caressing my breasts . . . enveloping me within his fingers . . . gently massaging my temples of thought . . . and penetrating my body with exotic lovemaking. I feel compelled to stay engulfed in this moment of blissful loving, but reality has set in now, and I realize that my imagination has gotten the best of me—and I am alone!*

*Alone, with the irony of masturbation to sulk in all of what I have just felt. I'm often reluctant to relieve myself of such feelings because of the loneliness that comes once it's over. I just want to slip back into the memories of yesterday's past. I want to go back to when I was in control. When I never knew what it felt like to have a man within my being—because when I do think about making love and those girlhood fantasies, it almost makes me regret becoming a woman. It never turned out the way I wanted, and of course, I never thought it would be like this.*

"Here I go daydreaming again. Let me give my girl Alanna a call. I haven't heard from her in a while and I really don't like being left out of the business. Hey Alanna?"

"Paris?" Alanna answers.

"Hey, sis, I am just going to get to the point. I was talking to Tameko, and she told me about the situation with Brian, Jennifer, and you."

"WHAT? Tameko told you?" Alanna exclaims.

"Yes, why are you so surprised?" Paris responds. "Was I not supposed to know?"

"Honestly, I didn't want anybody to know. It had nothing to do with you, Paris. Actually, I am surprised Tameko told you after I specifically told her not to say anything to anyone."

*She can't be serious. Alanna must be playing mind games,* Paris thinks, *because she knows Tameko and I talked.*

"I apologize that I didn't tell or come to you first," Alanna says. "I know how protective you are with us, but this was a stressful time for me, and it was a lot to deal with and hard to handle. My sister, Bri— anyway . . . *I am really happy you called. What's going on with you, Paris?*"

"Don't be coy with me, Alanna. I know you. You *knew* that I would call. Now, I want to hear it from *you* what's really going on. Start talking!"

"Nothing really," Alanna responds. "But I should have called, but it was hard, having to face reality. I was so ashamed and felt embarrassed."

"First of all," Paris says, "Alanna, you never have to feel alone. That's why we formed a sister club. So that the four of us—me, you, Tameko, Egypt—would always have each other to depend on. Do you remember, Ms. Lady?"

"Yes, I do, Paris," Alanna answers. "Honestly, Tameko just happened to call that day. She heard something in my voice, and we started talking. I just blurred it out. I didn't mean to keep it from you, Paris."

"A whole three months ago? This whole thing went down, and you never told me?" Paris tries to hide her disappointment. *It bothers her more than Alanna knows. Even if it happened so long ago and she just found out.*

"We all look up to you, and sometimes telling you stuff out loud is hard. We know you won't judge, but you will give your honest opinion, and it can come off as being harsh. I'm just saying," Alanna replies.

"WHAT! YOU'RE KIDDING ME, RIGHT? THAT'S BULLSHIT. DO ME A FAVOR, DON'T PATRONIZE ME. I am not hard to talk to, and I tell you guys everything the minute it happens, but I had to find out three months later. This doesn't make sense to me."

"You still see me as little Alanni. To you, I never grew up. You never accepted my womanhood, and it feels like I constantly must prove myself to you. I don't know why I feel that when I am a grown-ass woman!"

"Ha ha. I get it," Paris responds.

"Let's change the subject," Alanna says.

"First, Ms. Alanna," Paris replies, "I will never judge you. Not without looking at myself first. Second, I'm not a real friend if you can't come and talk to me about the smallest to largest things in your life. Being someone's friend also means accepting responsibility for the part you play. I love my friends. You guys are my sisters." Paris feels the tears coming.

"Hey, I'm really sorry," Alanna responds, also getting emotional. "I didn't realize how much this would bother you. I understand, and I promise to be more upfront with you."

"Okay. You better. You know, I am nosey when it comes to you ladies. We're family."

"I understand . . . no more secrets. Ha ha." Alanna smiles.

"Shit. I need a glass of wine after all that. You have any in the refrigerator?"

"Yes. Help yourself and pour me one too."

"Well, now, I guess I can bring you up-to-date with me as well. Recently, I was seeing this guy. I didn't tell anyone because it was a really difficult time in my life as well." Paris pauses.

"What do you mean difficult?" Alanna replies, intrigued.

"I guess that's why we haven't talked. I just got out of this relationship, guy named Mr. Leon Baker. We met down on the Fourth Ave. supermarket. He was charming, he approached me, and we just got into it."

"This sounds good already." Alanna smiles.

"Yeah, well, I wish. Not soon after getting to know him, he became abusive and disrespectful. He did a lot and he took a lot. I would have never left him if it weren't for Tameko. She came over while he was there today, and we got into it. You know Tameko . . . she got into his face, and the rest is history, and it gave me the strength to tell him to leave. I couldn't do it on my own. I was really scared, but Tameko helped."

"What? You! And with Tameko, I know his ass is out," Alanna states.

"Honestly, that was what I needed to get him out. I couldn't tell you ladies my story either. A man can get you to your lowest point and keep you there if you let him."

"Wow, I had no idea."

"And what made it worse is that, when Leon walked into my life, I had just gotten out of another relationship that I thought was good for me too. When a person shows up in your lowest point of your life, you know they are the wrong people to be around. If your energy is low, so is theirs."

"I don't follow, Paris."

"You will. It had something to do with a man who I really loved, but he hurt and disappointed me, and it drove me right into Mr. Baker's all-wrong arms."

"I think I get it. I understand why you spend so much time trying to protect your heart, and why your mind is always working overtime to explain the "The Reason", like the old song by Earth, Wind and Fire." Alanna laughs at her own reference.

"But I'm happy it's over," Paris replies. "It took a while. Hey, I forgot we were on the phone . . . do you still have time to talk? I can come over."

"Yes . . . of course. I'm just relaxing. Jennifer is at the store. She went to pick up some milk."

"Okay. I can be there in fifteen minutes. I have nothing planned to do. We need to catch up on some more stuff anyway."

"Okay, great. I'll straighten up, and I will see you then, but before you hang up, let me hear something you've been working on."

"I know, silly, here it goes, or better yet, let me text it to you. It's called 'Reasoning'!"

# REASONING

*What do I have to bargain with when I try to give you what you want?*
*Understand me if you can, you see being in your life*
*Has contributed to the woman I am, and sometimes*
*Those same contributions destroyed my focus.*
*I don't want to blame you*
*Because you led and I followed.*
*But loving you, suffice it to say,*
*Has blinded me enough to see.*
*I asked you to explain it to me,*
*To help me, and you say no!*
*There is no reasoning to understand this*
*And still, you will take from me, to glorify yourself.*
*This is not love to me.*
*But in your eyes, your way, I can still*
*Be loved by you . . . How? Please relate to me,*
*I can only give what you are willing to give to me. And I wait to receive*
*What you are willing to give, unselfishly. Love has no barriers or gates.*
*It is lavishly beautiful and uncontrollable giving of ones self.*

# SHE'S THE OTHER WOMAN

"Hey, girl. I brought a bottle of red. I know how much you like red wine." Paris enters the apartment. "I like what you did to your place."

"Yes, girl. I needed a change. Come on in and make yourself comfortable."

"Sorry, it's been a while since we last talked."

"I know, we all get busy sometimes. So, what's new with you?" Alanna asks.

"A lot, girl. Tameko just left my house."

"Oh, really, I didn't know she was going over there. I would have gone with her."

"I thought she would have told you."

*I need Paris to think I have no idea what's going on because if she knew I knew anything, she would have a fit.*

"Honestly, before I start with my stuff, catch me up with you. Tameko told me I need to talk with you about something."

"Yeah . . . she was right. We haven't talked in a while, but I wasn't trying to hide anything. It's just been hectic."

"I know and I understand."

"Hey, before we get started, let me pour a glass—do you want some? Are you hungry? I just made some salsa." Alanna goes to the kitchen to get the wine glasses and some snacks.

"Absolutely! Yes, I can eat. Even though it's early in the afternoon," Paris yells back.

"So, where do you want to start?" Alanna returns. *I know I am not ready to have this conversation with Paris, but it can't wait any longer. And now the cat is out of the bag, Paris is nosey as hell.* "Alanna thinks.

"You know, girl . . . it's better to start at the beginning."

"I heard that." Alanna relaxes, her feet on the couch as Paris begins.

*"There's always that one person who'll remind you of how/what love should feel like. It reminds me of moonlight dancing, a bouquet of juices flowing just for him. You know, on those rare occasions when I let my memories drift back, I'm reminded of, hmm, Mr. Joh Tomay. He was a tall, dark, and handsome guy with a smile to die for and a size fourteen shoe, need I say more?"* Paris reveals.

"No, I think I can visualize it. Wow!" Alanna responds.

*"He used to make me feel like a real woman. He treated me like the sun rose and shined around me. He used to say all the right things, do all the right things, and would even go with me—shoe shopping, hair, and nail salons—and wait until I was done! And believe me, there was no femininity about this man! He was in touch with his inner self, in touch with his manhood, too. He played his position well. And did I leave out, during my 'time of the month,' he would even go to the store for me, girl! He was heaven-sent. I never had a moment's concern when Mr. Tomay was around.* At least I thought."

"You thought? What? What happened? He sounds like he was Mr. Perfect." Alanna smirks. "As Tameko would say . . . Mr. Perfect Paris."

"Was, when, were! *Was* being the operative word," Paris responds. "Girl, I wish that were still so."

"Why? What happened?" Alanna says, surprised by Paris's hesitation. She sees how emotional this makes Paris.

"I remembered rushing home from work one evening because he had me wiggling in my chair all day. I couldn't sit still. I was on fire, dripping, panties moist just from the thought—the whole nine yards. I said to myself, 'Work isn't keeping my attention right now, and I need to go. I need to be with my man right now.' I left work early. And then I decided before going home, I would go to that market down on Fourth Ave., pick some salmon, salad, and a bottle of that white rosé we liked. I even picked up some rose petals. I was ready to get to the business."

"Shit, I would have been ready too," Alanna responds. "That sounds like a nice night along with personal dessert too."

"Well, as I am walking into the apartment—anticipating the moment of riding that golf pole," Paris adds with a laugh, "I was singing 'All I Want to Do' by Anita Baker. I sat the groceries down, hanged my coat, kicked off my shoes, took a quick shower, and walked into my bedroom room. Girl, I was ready to take care of business."

"*And?*"

"To my surprise I'm hearing strange noises. I couldn't place them at first."

"You're kidding me, right?"

"No, I am not. I went toward the bedroom, opened the door . . . "

"What happened? You dragging the story."

"My mouth was dry, the rage began to grow. I found the words, and I started yelling, screaming, I almost pounced on that ass, but I couldn't move."

"You are funny, Paris."

"This shit is not funny."

"I know. I am not laughing." Alanna smirks so Paris doesn't see her laugh aloud.

"This nigga was already taking care of business with someone else!"

"NO—are you saying what I think you're saying right now!"

"Yes! My Mr. Wonderful was in bed, all right! I found him in bed—with another woman!" Paris reveals.

"What? Paris! You're lying! Are you serious?"

"I wouldn't joke about something like that. I wouldn't lie about something like that, Alanna."

"I'm sorry . . . I . . . "

"*Yes, I was devastated. I was about to lose my damn mind. There I was, standing there, all wet and moist, feeling sure of myself, ready to get busy with a bottle of wine and rose petals, and girl . . .*"

"Girl. I don't know what I would have done." *Or maybe I do*, Alanna thinks.

"And here comes Mr. Tomay's head popping up from under the covers, in that all-too-compromising position that we women love."

*I know what you mean,* Alanna thinks out loud.

"Just thinking about how good that *shit* felt pissed me off even more," Paris states.

"OMG! Paris, I don't know what to say."

"All I could think was *That's my shit!* How dare she get some too? At that point, *all* hell broke loose. I couldn't believe it. I was on fire. All I saw was blood. I couldn't even cry, my red-bottom shoes flying, glass shattering. I missed his head with the bottle. I was trying to knock the *shit* out of him."

"Ah, ah, ah, I wished I could have been the fly on the wall." Alanna begins to laugh. "Please excuse me, Paris."

"Joh didn't realize I had entered the room until the shoes hit his ass in the head. Then I started throwing that bottle of wine, rose petals— anything I could get my hands on. He jumped up in surprise," Paris continues, "and looked at me like, *Oh shit! Damn, I got caught.* Then it became, 'Oh baby . . . oh, baby. I can explain, I can explain!' Seriously? How do you explain this shit?"

Alanna starts laughing again. "Excuse me. I am not laughing at you. It's just . . . "

Paris frowns as she watches Alanna holding back another laugh. "I don't see why your ass is laughing. We haven't gotten to your story yet."

"I know," Alanna responds. "And I don't mean to laugh, but . . . it's the way you're telling the story."

"Well, yeah," Paris admits. "Anyhoo . . . . . the next thing I knew I was like 'What the HELL is going on, Joh?' That's was all I could think. He kept saying, 'I can explain, I can explain, I can explain. It's not what you think.' And I was like, 'Are you serious?' I was about to leave the room and turned around. I forgot at that moment I was at my house. I about to leave my own home, when . . . 'It's *not what, you think,' Jon kept saying. It's exactly* what I think! All the while trying to put his pants on while jumping around on one foot, saying, 'Paris, wait, I need to talk to you.' And all the while I'm trying to get at this woman. She was trying to put on clothes as well and kept saying, 'I didn't know. Joh . . . who is this? You never told me you were in a relationship.'"

"I really didn't care about what she was saying. I could barely register her voice or anything she was saying. I was just trying to beat both their asses."

Alanna laughs again.

"I was doing my best not to cry," Paris continues, "but the tears . . . I tried to push them back. I didn't want this, this woman, to see me cry. They just fell. I guess it couldn't wait. As I was watching my whole life pass by me . . . here she comes with the bullshit. I was trying to give her the benefit of the doubt, and then here she comes and . . . "

"Really? What did she say?" Alanna asks.

"Well, it went something like this:

*'Joh? Excuse me, Joh?' the woman asks. 'Who's this?'*

I was like, 'Who is this? I am Paris, Joh's woman. Who are YOU? And what are you doing in MY house, in MY bed, and with MY man?'

The woman says, 'What? I'm sorry, but I didn't know he had a woman, much less bring to me to your apartment. I thought this was his place.'

'No, it's mine,' I say.

'I didn't know that . . . I would've never come to your house, and much less be in your bed! I asked Joh if he was married, in a relationship, if he had a boo, a wife, or a significant other. He told me no!'

'I . . . PARIS, PLEASE . . . ' JOH INTERRUPTS, STAGGERING AS HE FINISHES PUTTING HIS CLOTHES ON.

'NO, I'M NOT TRYING TO BE ANYBODY'S SIDE CHICK, THE OTHER WOMAN, SHE SAYS AS SHE TURNS TO JOH. 'YOU KNEW THIS FROM THE BEGINNING. I TOLD YOU, AND YOU ASSURED ME YOU WEREN'T IN A RELATIONSHIP.'

'BEGINNING?' I YELL. 'WHAT BEGINNING ARE YOU REFERRING TO? HOW LONG HAVE YOU BEEN SEEING EACH OTHER?' I ASK.

'Umm, she doesn't need to know all that, Sa—' Joh replies.

'Oh no! I *do* need to know. How long?' I ask again.

'Maybe she does. I don't want her thinking I'm some hoe, just laying up in bed with everybody's man!'

'I already think it,' I chime in, 'so don't bother with the details. It's already a thought . . . so . . . I'm going to ask you one more time: how long?'

'Six months!' the woman responds.

'More like four months,' Joh mutters.

'FOUR MONTHS? SIX MONTHS? WHAT'S THE DAMN DIFFERENCE? YOU MEAN TO TELL ME YOU'VE BEEN CHEATING ON ME FOR THE LAST SIX MONTHS, IN MY BED AND IN MY HOUSE? YOU'VE BEEN BRINGING WOMEN TO MY HOUSE ALL THIS TIME, IN THE SAME HOME WE'VE SHARED FOR THE PAST FOUR YEARS?'

'Four years?' the woman says, surprised.

'BIATCH! DON'T ASK ME _NO_ QUESTIONS. YES!' I YELL. 'I DON'T WANT TO HEAR ANYTHING ELSE FROM YOU! NOW . . . GET THE HELL OUT OF MY HOUSE, AND YOU CAN TAKE HIM WITH YOU TOO.'

'Excuse me—but I am trying to help you out,' the woman states.

'No, Paris, baby. You don't mean that. She doesn't mean anything to me . . . this is nothing!' Joh replies.

'Oh, now . . . she means nothing—that wasn't what it looked like fifteen minutes ago,' I say.

'NOTHING! I MEAN NOTHING NOW—REALLY! DON'T PLAY YOURSELF, JOH. I MEAN SOMETHING NOW, AND I MEANT EVERYTHING, EVERY WEEK FOR THE PAST SIX MONTHS. MY BILLS DID NOT GET PAID ON THEIR OWN, AND DON'T FORGET ABOUT THAT TRIP WE TOOK JUST LAST MONTH WHEN WE WENT TO THE DOMINICAN REPUBLIC. SO I AM NOT JUST . . . REALLY! You gonna try to play me because your ass got caught,' the woman states.

'YOU DID WHAT? This shit done went to an all new level. I'm sorry, but what's your name? Forget it! I don't need _to know your name!_'

The woman blurts out, 'Ah . . . ah . . . ah . . . it's Samantha.'

'Yeah, that's it,' Joh answers.

'You really tryin' it, Joh. You knew my name. Every time you came to my job, sent me roses, came to my house, paid my bills, and put my ass to sleep at night, etc.' She then turns around to me. 'Maybe you should know my full name. It's Samantha Jones.'

'What! You puttin' Biatches to sleep, really! You pay bills now, Joh? Wow . . . this is way too much. YOU NEED TO LEAVE—NOW. THE BOTH OF YOU CAN GET THE HELL OUT. YOU CAN HAVE HIM!

I DON'T WANT HIM. He can't do anything for me no more!'

'I DON'T WANT HER. PLEASE, PARIS! Just let me explain.' Joh turns around and tells Sam, 'Please . . . can you leave? I need to speak to Paris.'

*'No problem. I don't have time for this. This is crazy.' Samantha turns around as she is walking away. 'AS A MATTER OF FACT, LOSE MY NUMBER!' Samantha yells.*

*'Whatever!' Joh mutters. He puts his attention back to me. 'Paris, just give me a minute.'*

'DON'T SAY ANYTHING TO ME*! I AM ABOUT TO SLAP THE SHIT OUT OF YOU!' I respond.*

*'Oh! For a minute I thought you were talking to me. Not in this lifetime!' Samantha states. 'I know you're angry, but there will be no slapping here. Trust!'*

*'TRICK! IF I WANTED TO BEAT YOUR ASS, I HAVE EVERY RIGHT! DID YOU FORGET YOU ARE IN MY HOUSE, MY BUSINESS, AND SLEEPING WITH MY MAN!' I yell as I walk toward Samantha.*

*'No, no, no—sister girl. Keep talking crazy, and I just might beat your ass in your own house. Like I said, there will be no slapping or anything,' Samantha yells back.*

*'JUST LEAVE, SAM,' Joh says as he steps between us. 'No need to get violent. This . . . is my fault. JUST LEAVE, SAM! Please!'*

'Yeah! Sam . . . Samantha . . . slut . . . *whatever you call yourself. Get the hell up out of my house. Tramp!'*

*'Tramp? I'm nobody's tramp. Don't be mad* '_cause_ *you can't please your man, and he was spending your money on me.'*

'Whatever!' *I respond.*

'*Let me leave you with this—I didn't KNOW about you. I asked all the right questions, and he said nothing. You didn't come up in any of our conversations. So if you're really honest with yourself, ask your man about that,*' Samantha answers.

'*Well, he had it all, but that was up until fifteen minutes ago. He had a fiancée, a home, and anything he needed. We're done now! Take his ass with you.*'

'*Stop talking about me like I'm not here!*' Joh interjects. '*I'm standing right here. I can hear you. Paris, I love you. This— has nothing to do with us. She means nothing to me. It's over!*'

'*Now, WE'RE over, too!*' Samantha replies.

'*You've been cheating on me this whole time. Dang, I feel so stupid!*' I sigh.

'*Paris, baby, please . . . I lied,*' Joh admits. '*That's what boys do. We lie! It doesn't make it right, but I'm so . . . sorry! I am sorry. I know I hurt you. Just let me talk to you, Paris. Please!*'

'What about my apology?' Sam interjects. 'You lied to me as well . . . making me look crazy in these sheets.'

'Oh, yeah! Sorry, Pam—Sam, can you leave, now? So I can talk to my girl.'

Joh walks over to me. 'Baby, I'm sorry. I never meant to hurt you. I should've never brought my mess home to you either. And, for that, I am so sorry! You were always so busy. You never had time for me. A man gets lonely too.'

'*Oh! Now it's my fault. That you couldn't be faithful, committed?*' I reply.

'*No . . . it's not your fault, but like you once said, the loneliness gets louder than the words,*' Joh states.

'*THEN GET A HOBBY!*' I yell. '*HOW COULD YOU DISRESPECT ME LIKE THIS? HOW COULD YOU DISRESPECT OUR RELATIONSHIP LIKE THAT? I TRUSTED YOU! HOW MUCH IS ONE WOMAN SUPPOSED TO TAKE? THIS—WAS SO UNNECESSARY. DID YOU AT LEAST USE A CONDOM?*'

'*Please believe me. It meant nothing,*' Joh states.

Sam is almost out the door, but she turns around at Joh's words. 'NOW, I MEANT NOTHING BECAUSE YOU GOT CAUGHT? BUT WHEN YOU WERE CAUGHT UP, YOU SAID YOU LOVED ME! YOU WANTED TO SPEND THE REST OF YOUR LIFE WITH ME! ARE YOU SERIOUS?' SAMANTHA RESPONDS ANGRILY.

'I never said any of that to you!' Joh responds. 'I never told you I love you, and I never promised you anything. We had a good time, but now it's over. GET OUT!'

'You said you LOVED her?' I yell. 'If I hadn't walked in . . . it was already going on for a while. You probably said all those things to her. She's right, it's OVER because you got caught, Joh!' I say.

'Paris, baby, I know how this may look, but please talk to me. I have nowhere else to go!'

'As Halle Berry once said, "love should have brought your ass home". But then again, I guess it did. The joke's on me!'

'Go home with Samantha.' My voice rises. 'She'll have you!'

'Not!' Samantha responds. 'He can't come home with me. I live with my mother.'

'And this is what you cheated on me with?' I laugh.

'Sorry, but ah—my brother, but you're on your own. Bye! Oh, and Paris, for your information,' Samantha says as she opens the front door, 'Joh rarely used condoms. He hates them . . . isn't that right? Oh! Imma— send my brothers to kick your ass! Watch your back. It ain't over.' And with that said, Samantha walks out the door.

***

Joh tries to walk toward me. 'Paris . . . let's just talk it out.'

'It's over with us,' I continue. 'I never thought you would do this to me. I pride myself on the fact that I finally got it right. When all my friends we're male-bashing, I uplifted you. I vouched for you, I believed you, said all the right things. I even shared my finances with you! And this is how you repay me? And to think I was considering marrying you. I AM DONE!'

*'I never meant to hurt you,' Joh responds. 'I do love you, and I'll do whatever it takes to make this up to you. Call it being an ass, but I felt like I was missing out on something.'*

*'I hope you found it . . . it just walked out of the door!' I tell him as I start to cry. 'I gave you all of me! Everything!'*

*'I know, baby,' Joh says, close to tears. 'And . . . I am sorry. I'll make it up to you. No matter what!'*

*I walk toward the front door. 'Remember, what you do in the dark ALWAYS comes to light. You thought you wouldn't get caught. And on that note, it's time to go. Don't bother with your stuff. I'll mail your things, and the locks will be changed. I thought I could finally relax with someone. You don't deserve me.'*

*'Paris, please, baby.' Joh takes a step toward me.*

*'STOP BEGGING, MAN. IT'S OVER! Please don't call my job. If you call, I'll tell them to call the police.'*

Joh turns around and says, 'I love Paris Jones, and I am really sorry.' He walks out."

****

"Yep. That was my story," Paris concludes.

"Wow. That was a lot, Paris," Alanna says.

"That shit was crazy. I had to tell the story in real time, but it has been a while."

"I know, right? How long exactly?"

"I'm not sure, but it's been a while since I saw Joh, and I haven't seen Leon Baker either. As a matter of fact, I heard he's back in jail. His stupid ass went out and tried to rob someone. Remember, people always sending their representatives first. Sometimes all dressed up and looking good isn't always good for you—he wasn't who he appeared to be, either. In this conversation, this love thang is a lot to deal with."

"You're right. No one said it was going to be easy. How do you feel now?" Alanna asks.

"I'm a lot better," Paris admits. "Therapy is a good thing. I'm over most of it. If I can be honest, I admit, I miss Joh. Even though he cheated and after going to therapy, I realized, I had a part to play in it."

"What do you mean?"

"Through therapy, I learned I never made time for him, and we had some other issues like jealousy on my part."

"You? Jealous? I would never have thought." Alanna smirks.

"Anyhoo . . . it wasn't all his fault. I had my insecurities. Don't get me wrong, I don't condone cheating, but it takes two people in any relationship. We had a lot of good times before all this. If I ever get the opportunity, I need to apologize to him as well. Holding onto the past—I just needed to let it go. I'll do better for it."

"I hear that," Alanna responds. "And I'll remember that too. Do you still have time to talk?"

"Yes. Absolutely!" Paris responds.

"Okay. Before we get into it, let us take a coffee break, and in the meantime, you can recite me another one of them poems while I am walking into the kitchen. Let my living room be your stage. Take it away."

"Ha ha. Silly, girl. Here it goes. It's called 'She's the Other Woman'!"

# SHE'S THE OTHER WOMAN

*She is the other Woman!*
*She looks at me as though she knows me—but*
*Don't! Only, I know of her all too well, she is the other*
*Woman!*
*Who plagues my existence!*
*She rapes me, and she doesn't even know it and*
*She tells my story just by the strides in her walk.*
*As she approaches you, she knows only too well*
*How much you mean to me. Nonetheless, she*
*cannot and will not leave you alone!*
*Who is she? The other woman!*
*Because she knows, and she understands "exactly" why I stay.*
*The other woman has nothing to do with what*
*I don't need or have for you; she is just another hidden*
*Desire, you dared not share with me. Instead you keep*
*In a room all to yourself. Love, never that, lost or forgotten*
*Because I am "the woman," and "she is the other woman."*
*No contest, just the assurance of two women loving one man*
*All in one moment, a night, and now a lifetime.*
*Desperately seeking refuge from the deep furnace of your love.*
*She shares my understanding of loving you too hard and too strong,*
*Engulfed in the conversation, engulfed in the lovemaking,*
*I can now understand what it means to be the other woman!*

# MISGUIDED LOVE

As Paris begins to relax, a small smile comes across her face. This is the cue for Alanna to start her story.

"I am just going to get right into it. Don't be surprised by my entry. *When I found Brian in bed with Jennifer,*" Alanna begins, "I thought I would lose my mind. Why would he be sleeping with my sister after all I had told him? I started to notice subtle things about them, but I ignored it."

"Excuse me. Wait. Did I hear you right? Your sister, Jennifer?" Paris says.

"Yes. You heard me correctly. I found her in the bed with Brian. It was on a Thursday after working late. I came home and found them."

"How ironic." Paris smirks.

"The day I found my sister in bed with Brian . . . I was stunned, hurt, and disappointed. But in the end, I had to look at my contribution to the situation. My sister has had problems with men since we were children. It just wasn't clear until I came home that day, I realized how bad it had gotten."

"And your sister? Did she react, say anything?"

"Nothing! Not even 'I am sorry,'" Alanna replies.

"No . . . nothing. She didn't even cry?" Paris asks again.

"Nothing? Am I a damn owl? I said nothing," Alanna shoots back.

"I'm sorry, dumb question." Paris smirks.

"I'm sorry too," Alanna responds.

"It's okay. I get it. I was there too," Paris replies.

"So . . . what about Brian?"

"What about him? He took advantage of my sister. He knew she was molested as a child, and he knew because I told him. He also knew she had always been a bit promiscuous but innocently—I can't explain it, but it doesn't bother her at all. She needs help."

"I'm soooo . . . sorry!" Paris replies. "It's hard. I know!"

"My mother failed to see Jennifer's situation. Everyone thought she would have grown out of it, but she never did."

"Who's everyone?"

"I tried to get some help with the school therapist, but it didn't go anywhere."

"Sometimes, it's hard to see what is right in front of you. Being a parent, having to deal with a challenged child isn't easy. No matter what the capacity. Everybody got a story and a history too."

"I know my mother had a history of abuse and violence, and so I never faulted her, but it didn't mean she couldn't do anything about it, but she never said anything to Jennifer. I wished she had at least acknowledged it."

"This is hard, I know. I wish I could say something to make you feel better."

"I was just a child myself."

"You don't need to explain. I understand. So . . . back to your sister. Since then, have you been able to talk to her about Brian?"

"Honestly, Jennifer was only eighteen years old . . . she still doesn't get it. Know that it's a slow process. Plus, I've been protecting her for a long time."

"I'm so sorry. This is so different from my situation. There is no comparison." Paris embraces Alanna.

"Honestly, Brian knew what was up. I told him. For every woman or man who's ever been cheated on, it doesn't make it any easier when it's the person closest to you or someone you trust."

Paris can see the tears welling up in Alanna's eyes. "If this is still very painful for you, we can stop. If this is getting to be too much . . . " Paris lowers her tone to reflect empathy for Alanna.

"Honestly, it's all good. He apologized several times, but we couldn't get back together. I would never trust him again around my sister. And until I get help for her, I don't trust her around my men. I feel trapped in my own life. Dang!"

"WOW. I wouldn't either. I guess. Has it happened before? I mean the men you've dated?"

"No, not that I know of, but the truth is, something has been off for years."

"Well, how did you handle it? Did you beat her ass?" Paris aggressively asks.

"Excuse me! Not to be mean, but what did you do when you caught your man in the bed with another woman?" Alanna responds. "Did *you* beat her ass?"

"Touché, biatch . . . ha ha," Paris answers.

"Jennifer isn't emotionally available," Alanna continues. "As a matter of fact, she's nonresponsive to most stuff. I love my sister. No young child should lose their innocence like that, but this hurt on so many levels."

"It wasn't your fault, Alanna. I hope you're not blaming yourself. You did the best you could!"

"I did blame myself for a long time. I'm her older sister. I didn't protect her. My parents were always working. It was my responsibility, but I kept telling myself I was just a kid."

"You were just a child."

"It took a while, but I understand that now."

*Unfortunately,* Paris thinks, *this happens to a lot of young people.* "I commend you," she says aloud. "It must've been hard for you and your sister."

"At first it was because I couldn't comprehend her behaviors around men. It was almost like she welcomed the come-ons. It was 'misguided love,' and she never seemed to be bothered by any of it. She believed the men wanted her, and she pursued them. The therapist told me she just blocks it out, and when she's ready, she'll talk about it."

Suddenly, Paris holds up a finger—she hears someone in the other room. "Is Jennifer here, Alanni?"

"Yes, she is. But she can't hear us. The door is closed."

"Are you sure? We've been talking for a while."

"I told her you would be coming over, and we needed some time to talk. I asked her to not come out of her room for a while. She was watching a show on her computer. She has headphones on. It's all good."

"Really," Paris states.

***

Out walks Jennifer. "Hey, Aunty, Prissy," Jennifer states.

"Who you calling Prissy? Ms. Thing? *Should I* . . . how is my favorite big niece doing? I didn't know you were here I would have come into your room to say hello," Paris continues. "But your sister tells me you were watching a show."

"I was, but the show just went off. It's okay. Sissy told me you would be coming over and needed some time to talk."

Alanna chimes in now. "What's up? Are you getting ready to go out, and where are you going, Jen?"

"I thought I would go to the mall."

"Stop being overprotective, girl," Paris says. "She's a grown woman. By the way, Jennifer, are you okay? I . . ."

"She's just fine," Alanna answers quickly. "She's just going to the mall to meet up with her friends, right?"

"Don't forget, Aunty is always here for you," Paris says.

"Well, since you're here, can I get $50?" Jennifer says with a cunning smile. "I saw these new sneakers I want to buy."

"Sure, no problem. But your ass needs a job—you too big to be asking for money!"

"I've been putting in applications all over the place, but no one has called," Jennifer answers.

"She's has . . . but school has been tough, and with everything else going on, it's been a struggle," Alanna confirms.

"I'm confident someone's going to call soon," Paris responds.

"Thanks Aunty Prissy," Jennifer says with a laugh.

"Hey! You want my $50? Call me Prissy again."

"Ha ha. I'm sorry, I was just kidding," Jennifer states.

"I don't see your ass laughing now!"

"Make sure you call me when you're ready to come home. I will pick you up."

"That's okay, Sissy. I can get back on my own. You don't have to worry. It's still early," Jennifer replies.

"I know but I worry. So just call me anyway," Alanna answers.

"Okay. No worries," Jennifer responds.

"Bye, Aunty" Jennifer replies as she takes the money from Paris's hand. "I'll see you later!"

As Jennifer shuts the door behind her, Paris belts out, "Wow! She doesn't seem affected at all! I don't know what I was expecting, but I . . . "

"I know. That is what scares me. Jennifer does not seem affected or fazed by her behaviors with men."

"I'm sorry, I didn't realize how Jennifer doesn't show much emotion about anything."

"No, she doesn't, and I guess that is why I felt betrayed by Brian. He knew her history, and yet he let himself go too far with Jennifer. She may have a grown-ass body, but her mind is not fully developed."

"I get it and I understand. I would have felt the same way. Especially from my man."

"Anyhoo, trust me—I got this. I loved Brian, and he betrayed me and my sister's innocence. I resented my sister for a long time, but the doctor helped me to understand not only does she have a problem with men, but she may have a mental illness. They're still running tests, and it helped me to not blame myself or her for that matter. Yes, I am dealing with it, and my sister is getting the help she needs. Do you mind if I close this conversation for now?" Alanna adds.

"Okay, I understand," Paris adds.

"Sometimes it's a lot to deal with and talk about. I'm still getting used to it all."

"If you need me, I am here. I love you, Alanni. But after this conversation, I'm going to need another glass of wine," Paris jokes. "And of course, another poem! Let's just call it 'Misguided Love'!"

## MISGUIDED LOVE

*The presence of who you are*
*Is represented by what I wanted to see. It's not real.*
*It comes with the unknowing and the unassurance of what I*
*Could have received from you. You tricked*
*me into thinking I can love you.*
*You knew I don't know how, and I can't—but you pursued me anyway.*
*I don't want to do this, and I shouldn't have*
*stayed, but you made feel something*
*I'm not sure of. It's misguided love. It doesn't love me back,*
*and it can't promise me anything, but I want it anyway.*
*The thing is . . . it's playful and captivating to me*
*It teaches me I can play the game, too.*
*Only, the best part of this secret is between you and me—*
*I shouldn't, but I can't refuse you.*
*This Misguided Love is not mine to keep, and I know that now!*

# VULNERABILITY

"Did you ever see her again?" Alanna asks. After sharing a bottle of wine, the women's conversation had circled back to their failed relationships.

"I'm sorry . . . what are you talking about?" Paris asks.

"The girl Joh was seeing."

"Oh yeah. As a matter of fact, I did."

"How did you handle it?"

"I saw her once before down at the supermarket on Fourth Ave. I know she saw me because she started laughing. I should have slapped the mess out of her ass for real. *Not because I found in bed with my man but because she felt the need to rub it in my face.*"

"I understand."

"In the end, he did this on his own," Paris says. "There's nothing worse than being betrayed by the one person you thought you could trust. I hate it when women blame the other woman. But the truth is, he cheated while I was busy working—not sleeping around with other men. If I wanted to take some responsibility then, yes, I am very busy, because I'm a professional who works."

"I hope you don't blame yourself, Paris. It's not your fault."

"But that doesn't mean he can cheat whenever he feels like it or if an itch needs scratching."

"I hear that," Alanna answers. And then, after a pause, she asks, "Have you ever run into Mr. Tomay lately?"

"Not lately, but he calls from time to time, sends roses. I hang up, throw them in garbage. I'm not ready to forgive him. I was *good* for that man and good to him. He had it good and he knew it."

"So . . . why don't you change your number?" Alanna asks.

"Because it'll cost me money—and besides, I like the fact that he keeps calling and begging, even though I don't answer. Knowing Mr. Tomay, he'll get tired soon."

"You know what, Paris?"

"What?"

"Your *too* dang romantic and sensitive. I hope this taught your ass a lesson."

"And what would that be?"

"Be cautious and less submissive. Men have yet to learn that submitting to his woman is also growth."

"Alanna, like I said, you never would've suspected it: he was good to me, and he handled all my needs, inside and out of the bedroom, but anyway, getting back to you, baby girl. If you don't mind, let's change the subject."

"What's up?" Alanna feels a little vulnerable at this moment.

"I don't want you ever to think you can't come to me or talk about your skeletons. You can! Especially with me. I'll always be here for you. You'll always be my baby girl. But just so you know—I *do* see you — your womanhood's blossoming. I'll never disrespect or judge you on any level. Okay?"

Okay," Alanna responds. "I love you, Paris. I think we need to talk more often."

"You know, that's one our greatest faults. Talk more, less assuming," Paris says with a smile.

"I agree! But well, I guess that's enough conversation for me in one evening. Oh! Before I go, can I get my poem?"

"Yep. This poem reminds us that love has nothing to do with all of this, and just like men, we're all are vulnerable to the perils of relationships. Vulnerability blurs your vision and leaves questions. Here it goes. It's called 'Vulnerability'!"

# VULNERABILITY

*What can I say that doesn't make me vulnerable to you?*
*How do I express my thoughts without feeling that I'm less appealing?*
*I want to be all I can be, without feeling vulnerable to you.*
*I want to be confident and strong and less submissive to you,*
*Without fear.*
*I want you to see my passion, to live within my own realm of living.*
*But I can't. Because you find me a threat to you*
*And I am not.*
*You want to control my thoughts, my moves,*
*and give way, which leaves me*
*Vulnerable to you.*
*I want to get away from you, and yet you have control*
*Over me! Please stop!*
*I want to go away from you.*
*I want to be free, but I can't because you have made me*
*Vulnerable to you. I cannot breathe nor move.*
*I need to learn how to be strong and not . . . less of.*
*I can't trust my emotions anymore,*
*Which leads my path? I want strength and not*
*Vulnerability, accessible to you!*

# SILHOUETTES OF LIFE AND LOVE

"Speaking about men and women," Tameko says a few days later, talking with Paris over the phone. "I haven't seen or heard from Ms. Egypt lately. That girl knows she's about her business, her family, and her future. What were her children's names again? Oh yeah, Imani and Lashawn. Lashawn's going to be somebody's ballplayer one day. He stands six-five at fifteen years old. He's a great performer, gets good grades, and is well-mannered. As for Ms. Imani, she's so beautiful and tall just like her parents, but you know she's a teenage girl with a lot of sass. But I know Egypt, she's got that under control."

"Do you remember when we were in high school, and Egypt sampled some cocaine and nearly lost her mind? She was *so* paranoid and thought someone was chasing her. And not to mention she's a control freak."

"I remember, ha ha," Tameko states.

"She couldn't pull herself together, and I think that scared her. After that experience, Egypt got her act together and promised to never try drugs again. And to my surprise, she never did. I've always admired that about her. Egypt never strayed from her dreams, her goals. She remained steadfast and committed to what she wanted: a career and a family," Paris adds.

"Ian!" Tameko says abruptly. "That's his name, right? Egypt's husband?"

"Stop joking, Tam!" Paris responds. "You know Ian—they've been married for ten years now, but they've been together for fifteen, and—"

"Hold on!" Tameko interrupts again. "I've got someone on the other line. I'll call you later."

Paris hangs up the phone.

*Why don't I just give Egypt a call?* Paris thinks. *I'm sitting here, thinking my thoughts, thinking about the silhouettes of life and love and how it all plays a part in our everyday life of loving. All it takes is for the right somebody to turn your life around. As for Ms. Tameko, I don't know what happened to her. She became a tramp overnight—and she's proud of it. If she heard me say that, though, she'd be all upside my head. Let me give this girl a call.*

"Hey, Egypt. It's me, Paris!"

"Paris, dang girl!" Egypt replies. "I was just thinking about you and the girls, saying how we've been missing each other lately. We haven't talked in a while, more like two months?"

"That's why I thought I'd give you a call."

"Since I have you on the phone," Egypt begins, "I was thinking maybe we should have girls' night out?"

"Sounds like a great idea. Let me set it up," Paris states.

"Okay girl. Oh wait! *I got a call.* Call me back with the details. Lashawn's calling me." Egypt hangs up the phone.

*It'll be nice to be with all the girls for a change,* Paris thinks, hanging up the phone again. *A chance to hang out and do some drinks and just relax. Hopefully it'll go well, and we won't have to take Ms. Alanni home on our backs like the last time. Alanna knows she can drink. She can drink you and me under the table, even though she weighs no more than 125 pounds.*

*Here I go talking to myself again. I better stop before someone walks up behind and have my ass committed. They already think I'm losing mind around here. I just need a man around this stuff. It's getting lonely. Space is nice every now and then, but I'll admit, I don't need that much time alone. It's starting to drive me crazy . . . talking to myself . . . I don't know. Me time is over. What I need is about nine inches long, hard, and wide. I'm ready to get some "us time" going on. Let me give Tameko a call back.*

"Hey, girl . . . is everything okay?

"Tameko," Paris says, getting right to the point, "I thought we could do a girls' night out with the gang, like we used to."

"That sounds like a great idea. Did you speak with Egypt?"

"Yes! I told her I'd get back to her once I spoke to you girls. I thought we could go to a strip club or movie or something. Whatever you ladies want to do."

"First of all, Paris, I am *not* going to no strip club. I don't feel like seeing a bunch of men dangling their business in front of me."

Paris laughs.

Tameko continues to speak. "And then having to come home to an empty apartment and get into bed alone? I don't think so. Nope, not I."

"Here we go with the nonsense," Paris says as she rolls her eyes.

"What?"

"You *never* go home alone."

"Yes, I do—did! Whatever. Don't be jealous. Jealousy doesn't look good on you, Paris, baby."

"Okay," Paris says a little defensively. "So you think I'm jealous of you?"

"Yep. But you said it, not me."

"*Excuse me?*" Paris responds.

"Girl, please. Don't go getting your panties in a bunch. It's been three weeks, and a girl can get hungry. I need to drink," Tameko jokes.

"Just so you know, I'm not jealous and never will be. I've never been jealous of any woman."

"Whatever! Jeez, Paris. But hey, did you see that pimple on my face last week? It's been a minute."

"Yeah, I saw it." But under her breath, she adds, "You sure that's all it is?"

"Well, changing the subject—"

"Whatever girl—"

"Look! I'm not like you. I can't wait for months for Mr. Right to come knocking on my front door."

"Like me?"

"Yes! Like you, Paris."

"It's not easy, but a good dildo, a movie—I make it work!"

"Really. Eel!" Tameko responds.

"Don't act like . . . you didn't put me on to the movie and a dildo. Tameko. I was a prude for a while, but I got into the game. Like I said, I maybe alone but I am not lonely . . . ha ha."

"I'm sorry, Paris. I didn't mean it like it sounded." Tameko smiles.

"It's okay. I know you meant well, Tam."

"Paris," she continues thoughtfully. "I didn't think you cared about my sex life."

"I really don't, Tameko. But I *do* care about my best friend."

"We all got stories to tell about yesterday's past. Dang, Paris! You take things too seriously! And besides, I talk a big game, but I don't always act on it."

"Yeah, right! Knowing you, Tameko, you'll do anything if you can get away with it. I remember when you caught that venereal disease in high school, and you hid it for nearly *three weeks* before you acted on it. You couldn't damn near sit down. It was only because you got sick . . . and the smell—*Lord, chile*! I don't know what took you so long."

"Dang girl, did you really have to remind me?"

"I am sorry . . . not to throw daggers . . . I was saying."

"I remember," Tameko says, "but we're all grown up now. Besides, there's a lot more precautions out there now. You *would* remember that mess! On a much lighter note, though, I would never disrespect our friendship like that. I would never put you in a compromising position where you'd have to rescue me. I love you like a sister, Paris. So . . . what about you? What's been going on with your poetry lately?"

*There she goes, trying to change the subject, that's my queue . . . it's time to go,* Paris thinks. "I'm still writing, girl. I'm still trying to find my way. My craft is a little rusty, but nonetheless I'm still walking the pavement."

"Well, before I go . . . do you have any stuff you want me to read?"

"As matter fact, yeah. And it would fit our discussion today. It's called 'Silhouettes of Life and Love.'"

## SILHOUETTES OF LIFE AND LOVE

*Walking in the shadows of life*
*Straining and dreaming of silhouettes.*
*Moments of when it became crystal clear.*
*Tarnished by the loves that have come and gone*
*Only to leave the memories of tears*
*Salted by the water that glazed my cheeks.*
*I've come a long way to change and mature*
*Into the woman I know, she has loved and lost*
*In the same existence of who she has become.*
*I want to know her; do you know her?*
*She is your mother, friend, and lover.*
*She is you. Smile when you think of her*
*Love her when you see her. But most of all, embrace her*
*Because she walks with a glow of light that transcends*
*Down from up above.*
*Oh, I'll walk slowly, because I hope to become her friend.*
*Lover of life! Smile when the petals of rain and the snow glisten*
*My face because I now know and understand her strength to travel*
*On this strange road we call "life and love."*
*Slowly life has taken me, but I'm ready, willing, and able to develop into*
*the thoughts of how and what we love to see, excelling, inspired by*
*You, and how you make me feel.*
*I'm flowing through you; I encourage, empower you.*
*The silhouettes of life and the joy of love*
*I now offer unto you!*

# LOOKING AT OLD TIMES

*There goes my phone again*, Paris thinks, waking up from her nap. *Dang! I can't get a moment's rest. Who could this be?*

"Hello, hello?" she states. "Who's this?"

"It's me, Massai . . . hello . . . . hello."

"Yeah," Paris says with a frown. "I only know one person named Massai."

"Yes, it's me. Dang, girl, what's wrong with you? You sound angry."

"I was just trying to get some sleep. Hey, what's up? I wasn't expecting any calls. When did *you* come home?"

"I've been home for about three weeks now. It's good to be home. I've really missed being out in the community. Seeing old and new friends."

"Oh, I see."

Massai noticed Paris's agitation. "What's wrong with you, girl? It's been a minute. I know you might not want to talk to me, but I've missed you, girl. And I just wanted to know how things are going. I've been looking all over town for you."

As Massai talks, Paris begins to regret acting so cold toward him. *I've missed Massai. He still has an effect on me,* she thinks. "Apparently, you haven't been looking hard enough because my number hasn't changed, and the address is still the same. Man, please!"

"Wow, okay. I wasn't expecting that—but then again, I was."

"You know, you're gonna have to come a little better than that, Massai."

"You're right, Paris. I'm sorry. I forgot who I was talking to."

"I'm sure."

"It's just that we left things on a bad note, and I didn't know what to say to you . . . or better yet, what I *should* say."

"If you really wanted to know how I felt, been, and what was going on with me, you would've called. You call yourself a man, yet you're still running, Massai. Please."

"Excuse me? I know it's been a minute, and I understand you're angry, but what you *won't* do is disrespect me. I'm a man in every sense of the word. Believe *that*!"

"Whatever!" Paris replies.

"Whoaaaa . . . I'm sorry, I thought we had a friendship. I thought this part of us would have never changed. Maybe I was wrong to assume. Even though it's been a while, I didn't expect this . . . maybe this was not the right time to call. Paris, I . . ."

"What?"

"Let me start by saying . . . we were young, and I take full responsibility for not being around and never giving you my time. I was selfish back then. I was emotionally unavailable to you."

"Really . . . Unavailable, to say the least. I really liked you . . . cared about you, but I just thought you toyed with my emotions, Massai."

*"Naw—I never played games with you. Honestly, I just wasn't ready, and I wasn't brave enough to tell you, Paris."*

"I thought we talked about everything. I thought you were my person. I trusted you! So don't talk to me about respect. I didn't get that from *you*." Paris's voice rises.

"DO YOU WANT TO HEAR THAT I MESSED UP?" Massai states.

"Who you are raising your voice too, Massai?" Paris asked.

"I am sorry, Paris," Massai states.

"Whatever!" Paris responds.

"Okay, I messed up! After I promised you, I was getting myself together! I was going to do the right thing this time. I thought so. I wanted it too. But I wasn't ready."

"I was here waiting for you to choose me. Choose us! There was always something keeping us apart—the streets. A woman can never compete with the streets. It will always outrun her."

"You think it's easy being from the streets? The truth was, I loved the streets. It was the only place I felt I belonged."

"AND WHAT ABOUT ME?" Paris yells.

"This had nothing to do with you. It's a man thing. I knew I wasn't ready to give it up, not even for you. I just wasn't ready. You're a woman, and you will never understand the adrenaline the streets gives us. It talks to you, and you run to it. You can't know the feeling," Massai states.

"You right, I don't, but it's all good now," Paris states.

"I honestly didn't think I was ever going back to jail, never! I genuinely wanted to be part of it . . . of something! The choices I made may not have been right, but it felt right for me in the moment. I got a natural high from just being involved."

"You're right! It *was* always about you—and *only* you!" Paris exclaims. "You left me out here. As long as I can remember, that's exactly how it's been—about *you*."

Massai hears the anger in Paris's voice, and it catches him off guard. "Hey, hey, I owe you an apology. I don't think I ever told you . . . how important you were to me Paris, and I honestly couldn't. Paris! Really, baby. I'm sorry. I'm surprised. I had no idea you felt so strongly."

"It's all good. I was finally able to *get it* out, and I feel better now. I'm okay, Massai."

"Look . . . I just came home. This has been the longest time I've been down, but this time, I'm finished. There will be no more going back to jail. I've been reformed."

"I've heard that before," Paris replies.

"You're right! You have heard it before. This time it's the truth. I didn't want to look into your eyes and lie again. I didn't want to disappoint you one more time, so when I came home this time . . . I just avoided you altogether. Believe me when I tell you it didn't make it any easier to deal with—at least that's what I thought. Girl, I never forgot about you. And believe me when I tell you, I kept an eye on you from the inside."

"You did?" Paris says, surprised. "And how'd you do that?"

"You graduated from college. A lawyer now! Are you're still writing poetry? You used to write some serious stuff."

"Thanks. I'm still at it," Paris tells him. "So what do you want? Massai?"

"What makes you think I want something?"

"Because I only hear from you when you want or need something!"

"Paris, a lot has changed. I'm no longer that money-grabbing, selfish, conniving, egotistical . . . are you going to stop me?" Massai states with a laugh.

"No, you're doing just fine," Paris adds.

"Oh well. Let's just say the 'street person' you used to know is gone. It's no longer here. Honestly."

"Talk is cheap but being responsible, considerate, thoughtful . . . Those were some of the qualities you seemed to fall short of, Massai."

"But I thought I always had the privilege of calling you and just saying hello. And I've never *asked* you for anything—except your friendship and respect! Paris, I admit I messed things up between you and me. You were the only thing in my life that was going right. I was just moving too fast and didn't take the time to slow down."

"I understand, and you're right, a lot has changed," Paris adds.

"I thought I'd be missing out on something in the streets but in the end . . . I missed out on the only thing that mattered: the people I loved. I messed up when I lost you. If I knew what I know now, I'd give anything to go back to the time of holding you and making plans," Massai replies.

"Yes, we were young back then . . . " Paris relates.

"We were. I was foolish . . . " Massai smiles.

"I know what you mean, Massai. I'm not going to lie, being with you was some of the best days of my life. I'll hold them in my memories forever," Paris admits. "Just before you called, I was thinking about the old times. I still remember when we looked into the future and dreamed about the tomorrows to come, never understanding the 'subliminal messages' that lies ahead. But for us, together, tomorrow never mattered."

"I know what you mean," Massai responds. "I'll always hold on to those moments, too. That's the problem with being locked up. You lose a lot. To some of us, it matters, to most of us, it doesn't. *That* is how you survive inside the brick wall."

"The woman I am today," Paris continues, "wants to be so sure of herself—but she sometimes has doubts too. My mind sometimes drifts back to a time when I . . . we . . . but that doesn't matter anymore."

"Yesterday past and present," Massai replies, following Paris's train of thought. "Moving toward new beginnings . . . allowing me to get caught up in the simplicity of life . . . things have gotten away from me, too."

"I didn't know you were a poet." Paris smiles.

"Nah, not at all. But I picked up some things while I was away. Just know, I understood you, girl, even back then just as I do now. Men have dreams, but the code in the streets is never to show your inner feelings—or else you'll end up getting punk or snuffed. Being inside the concrete walls, you'll hear in the quietest moments the many tears being shed—for lost ones, loved ones you'll never see or touch again. The loved ones being left behind due to the ignorance of the lost souls in the night. I understand your need to be loved, and I wanted to be the first person to lay hands on you. Upon that sweet, beautiful, innocent body of yours, and to drink the scent of your body oils. But I got complacent early on."

Paris is speechless, frozen. This is not the man she remembered.

"What I had to learn," Massai continues, "was that I played a part in our failed generation. And if we continue to act in such an immature manner, the young people of today will have nothing to look forward to. *I played a big part in this decision, and it's only now that I understand my position on this journey we call life. So from this moment on, I can only extend my hand to those who need it. I wish . . . not only did I fail you, but I failed myself as well. And I understand now! The moment I failed to see how important our relationship was, was the moment I failed to make you understand your beauty as a woman.*"

"I know how you feel," Paris says, recovering her voice. "We, as women, also have lessons to learn. Especially because we're also guilty of pushing our men out of our lives, or of treating them as if we don't need them—only to end up becoming lonely women."

"Baby girl, I see you're still profoundly serious and passionate about what you want. That's one of the qualities I could appreciate about you. You always kept it real. And for the record, don't think no one could understand you—I could! Remember, there was a brother named Massai who truly loved you, girl."

"Did you ever really love me, Massai?" Paris holds her breath, waiting for his answer as if—suddenly—it's the only thing that mattered.

"Yes. I never told you, but I really did. That's what happens to a brother who has no time to slow down, or to tell those who really matter to him what's on his mind."

"You know, Massai, I really needed to hear that."

"I'm happy that I'm still here for me to tell you, Paris. And I'll always love you, girl. My time is done. No more going back to jail. Maybe I'll write a book about the streets and the concrete wall. It's no place for a brother to end up, and it's definitely no place to call home."

"I hear that," Paris replies.

"If you want to take some time to get to know a brother again, you'll know where to find me. I'll be at my mama house until I get my situation situated."

"Well, Massai, I hope it all works out for you this time. Not to be rude, and please don't misunderstand, I've moved on. Life waits for no one."

"You're not rude, Paris. I *do* understand," Massai replies.

"I'm sorry, but I can't give you any more of my life. So . . . before I go, let me tell you—*thank you*. I deeply appreciate this call."

*Dang,* Massai thinks, *that girl still got it! I messed up big time. But like she said, life waits for no one.* "Maybe we'll do this again sometime," he says aloud. "For right now, though, I hope you got a poem for me. Just for old time's sake?"

"For you, Massai, I think I have something just right for us. Selah."

# LOOKING AT OLD TIMES

*Looking at old times, I knew you would return.*
*How could it, would it be possible to stay away?*
*Some say we've changed, but I can still see*
*You in me, and how we've come to be who we are today!*
*You see, walking away meant losing you altogether*
*And I couldn't afford that—to stay and lose me too! So I walked away.*
*It's so good to see you grow and become what I know.*
*I dreamt of what this day would bring, for you to stay, to stay,*
*Here with me forever.*
*If there's an "ever between us"!*
*The future is now upon us, and yet the past is there, too. Let me go*
*For the last time, this time, never meaning to*
*return. You're not mine to keep.*
*And yet I feel no sense of leaving you again, never!*
*Loving you, cherishing you,*
*Together we are making plans, understanding*
*my plan to see you, again, and again.*
*Forgive me! . . . I just can't walk away!*

# SURRENDER

"Hello, Alanni," Egypt says on the phone.

"Who is this strange voice?" Alanna answers. "I haven't heard that voice in a minute."

"I know, that's right," Egypt replies. "Where have you been? It is nice to hear from you. It's been a while."

"I'm sorry, I know," Alanna responds. "We'll have to work on that."

"I was calling because I have not heard from Paris all day. Have you heard from her?"

"Yes. The last I heard, she was going to the gym after work."

"Yeah . . . but that was hours ago. Now it is after eight o'clock at night. I'm starting to get worried."

"Paris is a grown woman, and she can take care of herself, mother hen!" Egypt accuses.

"Yeah, well . . . it's not like her to not check in. She is trying to get her head straight after the breakup with Joh. Leon was just a bad distraction who turned out to be a nightmare. Now, all of a sudden Massai calls after all these years. It's got her head all twisted, and she's just trying to put everything back into perspective."

"I can't argue with that," Egypt replies. "I thought she'd never get over Massai. But the day Mr. Joh appeared—he was a good distraction from Massai. When Massai left, it really hurt, Paris. You knew when she loves, she loves deep and hard. Besides, the dating game is difficult. It seems impossible to find someone you can communicate with or even be compatible with."

"How would *you* know, Egypt? You have been married for over ten years and appear to be happily married to a wonderful person and father, but something tells me you are not feeling it lately. I feel like something is off with you guys. What's up?"

"You're right. I have no idea. I should be grateful every day, and appreciative of what I have . . . I . . . "

"Yes," Alanna says, equally distracted. She returns to the conversation. "I . . . what? What are you talking about, Egypt?"

"Well, since *I* got you on the phone, Alanni, what's been going on with you?" Egypt asks.

"You still call me Alanni? You know we are not kids anymore."

"No. But old habits are hard to break, and yes, you are all grown up but, you will always be my Alanni. As for my family and ah . . . husband. . ." *Dang,* Egypt thinks. *I hope Alanna did not catch on to that hesitation in my voice.*

"I caught that 'ah . . . husband,'" Alanna repeats. "Why do you sound so iffy suddenly? You knew you lucked up when you married that Ian."

"I know, I know, girl. Honestly, I also know how hard it is to find a good, decent, caring man—I do! But still," Egypt confesses, "I'm not as happy as I once was."

"What are you talking about, and wasn't it you just running on about how *lucky* you are?"

"Yes . . . but . . ."

"But! But what?"

"I don't know," Egypt responds. "Ian is starting to get on my nerves. He is boring, in and out of the bedroom, he does not excite me anymore. I do not know. Maybe it's me!"

"Maybe it is that seven-year itch, or in your case, a little more, give or take. It takes work, and I am sure if you speak with Ian . . . he will work on it. It just takes a little conversation," Alanna states.

"He just . . . I do not know," Egypt replies.

"Gets on your nerve. How so? I wish I had someone to get on *my* nerves." Alanna responds.

"I don't know, but I feel like I'm missing out on something. It has been ten years—and if you count time during the dating stage, let us just say it's been longer than that," Egypt states.

"Why does your voice sound crazy to me?" Alanna asks, worried about where this conversation is going. "Like you're thinking about doing something *other* than being faithful to your husband?"

"I'm not . . . I . . . I don't know!" Egypt replies, frustrated and confused.

"Let me repeat myself: I *know* you're not thinking about slipping out on your husband if that's what you're proposing. I am here to tell you—do not! You have no idea what is on the other side of the grass. It is not always greener on the other side. Think about what you're thinking very carefully. Here I am starting to sound like Paris," Alanna exclaims.

"Yes. You do . . . it's crazy, I know." Egypt smirks.

"You're looking crazy to me right now, Egypt!" Alanna answers.

"I don't think I want to cheat, but I'm feeling so many emotions all at once. I just wanted to talk to you about my feelings. Honestly, though, it did cross my mind."

"To cheat? Go ahead. You will regret it. Don't! It is not worth it."

"And lately, I am so emotional," Egypt responds.

"Please think before you react because you don't want to be the wife running back home, begging your husband to take you back. You are allowing ants to get inside your heads."

"Ants?"

"Yes, another negative thought, because your thoughts lead you down the wrong path. You never know what is waiting for you on the other side. You remember Sparkle. Our childhood friend. She cheated, and he gave her something she'll never forget: AIDS."

"I remember . . . silly girl, ha ha. Not that it's funny, but I get your point. It is just that Ian stopped doing all the little things that made me feel special," Egypt explains. "It's not the lovemaking. It's the little things."

"Like what?" Alanna asks.

"The romance is missing. Something has changed. Ian is all work and no play, and he is becoming a bore. I am still very much in love with this man, and I *know* he loves me but . . . girl! I need some more attention—playtime—something!"

"Like David Hollister said, you had better take care of home, or somebody else will. Are you looking to add some spice in your relationship?" Alanna questions.

"Like what?" Egypt asks.

"Maybe another man or woman?" Alanna says with a laugh.

"I am strictly dick-ly. Shit—I'm not crazy, just a little bored."

"Well . . . good. You were beginning to make me concerned—"

"Hold on, Alanna," Egypt interrupts. That's my other line."

"Hi. It's me," says a new voice.

"Me who?" Egypt asks.

"Paris?"

"Hey, girl, sorry I couldn't catch your voice. Where have you been all day? Alanni was getting worried," Egypt says, raising her voice.

"You still call her Alanni?" Paris asks.

"Yes, yes, 'til the day I die. Anyway, hold on so I can put you both on three-way. Alanni is holding."

"Hello? Alanni, you still there?" Egypt says as she plugs the call.

"Yes. What took you so long?" Alanna voice rises.

"Paris is on the phone . . . Paris, are you there?"

"Yes," Paris replies.

"Good," Egypt responds. "You both here?"

"Yes!" Alanna and Paris answer at the same time.

"Tell Paris! Tell Paris what your ass is thinking. I bet you she is going curse your ass out. Go ahead tell her," Alanna says, raising her voice a little.

"Tell me what?" Paris asks.

"Tell her, Egypt, or I will!"

"*What* is going on? What should I know?" Paris asks, curious now.

"Wait 'til you hear this bullshit, Paris," Alanna says.

"I'm . . . well . . . I'm thinking about maybe having an affair," Egypt blurts out.

"What? How and with who? I *know* . . . I didn't just hear you say you want to have an affair. *Please* tell me I didn't just hear some bullshit like that. Egypt?"

"Honestly, it was just a thought . . . I did not anticipate acting on those feelings. I just don't know."

"You don't what? You better find out what you don't know with your husband. You think you want to be single until you are. It is hell. It is lonely, and most of the time, you sit in your thoughts. Alone!" Paris says.

"I know. I heard it all from Alanna," Egypt responds.

"No, baby girl," Paris continues. "You have no idea, but if you want to give him away, someone will be happy to take him from you. You see, women like you always get the good dudes. You use them, get tired of them, wanting to be with someone else, throw them away like some unwanted trash."

"I never said I did not want him. I am just bored, that is all."

"No matter how you put it, Egypt. It is the same thing. You know what they say, a woman's trash is another woman's glory. Let him go if you want to. Some other woman will scoop him up. He is a good man, a hard worker, easy on the eye, and he smells good. Shit, now that I think of it, I want him."

"You would date Ian, Paris?"

"Hell yeah. That is a good dude."

"That's some white woman shit. They do not care. Sister or not, they will date your man right in your face."

"Call me white then. I am coming for him, especially if you don't want him. He is not a bad look. If he weren't like a brother . . . I'd take him myself."

"Tell her, Paris!" Alanna nods.

"Whatever, I am not listening to y'all anymore."

"You had better take me seriously. I am not joking, and I gave you the heads up. Keep playing," Paris adds.

"We can close this subject. Moving on," Egypt states.

"I thought so because you are just talking out the side of your face. Let us get back to what's essential. What's wrong with you, Egypt?"

"You would never understand, Paris."

"Try me. Maybe I will."

"Okay. I've been feeling a little lonely lately. More like neglected."

"Your ass needs a hobby or something? Or *maybe* it's the ten-year bug? Trust me. You have no idea what is waiting for your husband out there. The ratio is ten to one. Including me. Act like a fool if you want to. You'll be crying for your husband to come back home," Paris adds.

"I knew you'd never take my side on this," Egypt replies.

"This isn't about sides, Egypt. This is about you being selfish. You're not considering your family," Alanna adds.

"We've been married for over ten years, and I'm beginning to think I'm missing out on something. I want more!" Egypt states.

"It seems like you are the only one who craves more, and what does 'more' look like to you since you want it so bad?" Alanna interjects.

"Let me tell you something, Egypt," Paris begins, "there are women looking, needing, trying to find a man. You are just lusting after a man! Do not be a fool. Sit Ian down. Help him to see your vision and where you want this marriage to go."

"Maybe create a few romances for him," Alanna interjects.

"You know, we think the man has to be the only one to creating all the moments or activities, but it takes two to sustain a relationship."

"I hear you, Paris," Egypt responds.

"Shit, do a bar scene," Paris continues. "Do whatever it takes to save your marriage. The winters are cold, and nights are long. Pillows do not suffice. Girl . . . you will miss his belly warmer, and trust . . . he will have no problem finding a warm blanket this winter."

"As Paris stated before, women are waiting for him, including me, and I'm going to be like the white girls. This has nothing to do with friendship, and we can still be friends and drink tea together, but I am going to get it. Believe that!"

"You would really date my husband if you had the chance?" Egypt asks, surprised.

"Hell yeah!" Paris replies. "At that point, he is no longer your husband. You gave him away. He is a free man. Moreover, I already know him, so we do not have to wait too long. If you know what I mean. Ha ha."

"Biatch, do not make me come through this phone and whip your ass. Ian is still my husband."

"Who you mad at? You do not want him," Paris explains.

Alanna laughs.

"Why should I suffer? Girl, be sure about this next move. He's a goddamn commodity!"

"You're crazy," Egypt says with a laugh.

Alanna answers. "The problem is . . . you think it's a joke, but she's not kidding. She's warning you!"

"Okay, okay, enough about my husband and me," Egypt says, moving the conversation in a different direction. "What else has been going on with you, Paris?"

"Not a whole lot," Paris responds, but in her head, she is thinking, *Let him go if she wants to, and when she does, I'll be the first in line!*

"Since we are talking about boyfriends, husbands, I heard Massai is back in town, and he called you!"

"Dang, Alanna!" Paris immediately snaps back to the conversation. "You can't keep a secret!"

"There *are* no secrets in the girls' club—remember?" Alanna responds, quoting Paris's own words back at her.

"It's just like you to keep *your* secrets from us, but then want *us* to tell you everything!" Egypt says. "Spill your guts, Paris!"

"There's not much to tell."

"Who's being selfish now?" Alanna responds. "You told me Massai had *just* called."

"He did what? Ms. Girl!" Egypt acts surprised even though she already knew Massai had called.

"I told him I wasn't interested, and that I'm not willing to go there anymore with him."

*"Go back to where?"* Egypt asks.

"It's just like him, thinking I am sitting around here waiting for him to return, come home to me."

"Are you?" Alanna asks.

"No. I am not. I waited a long time for Massai to return, show up and be the man I needed, but that never happened. We are done. It is over."

"I remember when he could make you *laugh!*" Alanna says, and Egypt laughs aloud with her.

"You're right, ladies, but that was many moons and many tears ago. And I have grown since, and I'm a better person because of it. I want this year to bring forth a whole lot of happiness for me. I want to attract the right man. But in the meantime, I'm doing me."

"I like the sound of that. I'm doing me too," Egypt affirms.

"Let me worry about my husband. Do you have a husband, and when you get one, we can talk about my ten-year itch and so forth?"

"No, biatch, you had better do Ian. Stop playing," Paris adds.

"Moreover," Alanna chimes in, "it looks like you need to back off, Paris. Momma getting made."

"Touché," Paris adds.

"We *all* need to do us. But dang, Paris, we've all heard your 'I want a man' speech. We know it, we heard it, and we don't care to listen to it anymore."

Alanna thought she would beat Paris to the punch line. "You're starting to sound like a broken record," she concludes.

"Girl, be quiet," Egypt says, coming to Paris's rescue.

"You better stop babysitting your little/big sister and go out and find you somebody."

"Whatever, Egypt. We good."

Paris smiles at Alanna's words but does not pay much attention to them. *Alanna is still young and naïve about life and things,* she thinks.

"At least *I'm* getting some on the regular," Alanna adds.

"With *whom?*" Egypt and Paris yell at the same time. Alanna had not said a word about a new boo.

"It's for me to know and you to find out," Alanna says evasively and then changes the subject. "You know, Paris, you've always had a way with words."

"I guess we are changing the subject now. Thanks, Alanna," Paris replies. "I just need to be patient and surrender!"

"I've heard you both and am going to work on it, too. Especially now, I know Paris wants my man. Ha ha. I need to talk with Ian."

"Absolutely! I do. You had better learn how to surrender," Paris says thoughtfully. "I wrote a poem on that, and I think it will fit this conversation, Egypt. Maybe you can read it to Ian. And help him understand the new you."

"I think that is a good idea," Alanna responds. "You are always leaving us with words of wisdom."

"Well, I'm going to go, ladies," Paris says. "I need to get in the shower and finish taking care of *me*."

"Ha ha. I heard that," Alanna adds.

"Ha ha. You crazy real with it. So before you go, let me get that poem from you," Egypt says.

"I don't have it right now, so I'll just send it to you. I can trust you with my words."

"Of course, silly. With your life!" Egypt adds.

"That's why I love you, girls. Good night!"

"Bye, big sis," Alanna says.

"Bye, my love," Egypt says while trying to process the whole conversation. I needed that—a reality check.

*Paris is coming for my man. Ain't that some shit. Biatch sounds serious too. Maybe it is time we all did some soul-searching,* she thinks. *Paris is right—it's about to bleed this winter, and I need to be lying next to my warm blanket, doing a lot of pillow talk.*

Meanwhile, Paris's mind is already back on her poetry. *It's called "Surrender." I have not read this one in a while. If I remember, it went something like this.*

# SURRENDER

Some say I've changed
Nevertheless, I question them to see
The shapes of objects that surround
Me.
I have grown, I know, because of you,
I surrender unrelentlessly before you.
She has come full circle—from the person
She once knew, only to arrive at the woman
You shaped.
I challenge you to take me there,
To the place, we succumbed together.
I completely submit to you, "Me," now!
Your vision is mine; it is I you've come to see
You made me, and now you don't recognize your
Prize, oh how wise, I am still by your side.
Anchor me, adore me. What do I have to do?
I owe you, Me but not all, because I'm me.
That woman you adored to see, so profoundly beautiful,
It is you in me that you've come to see, I surrendered.

# EMOTIONAL LOVE

*I really need someone to talk to right now. Let me give Egypt a call. I just need to let off some steam. How many times does the phone have to ring before she picks up? Egypt better be home,* Paris thinks.

"Hello?"

"Hi, Egypt . . . this is Paris. I really need someone to talk to right now. Are you available? This can't wait. I am having a moment. Do you mind?"

"Not at all," Egypt replies.

"You know, I was thinking back to an old conversation and remembering my mother at the same time: we used to talk about emotional love."

"Emotional love? That sounds heavy. I can only imagine the flow of that conversation," Egypt says.

"Yeah. It was heavy, but my mother was an analytical thinker," Paris says. "But I could never really get a handle on it. She talked about that "love" that never leaves your soul. It's always there, and when it shows up, you feel it all over again."

"Where is this coming from?" Egypt asks.

"I guess I'm just reminiscing about when it comes over me. The rain is falling from the sky without notice. It just came to me, and the first person I wanted to call is you. I wrote this poem called 'Emotional Love,' and as I think about it, I think back to when I was a child and what emotional love did to my mother, my siblings, and our family."

"What do you mean?" Egypt inquires.

"I watched emotional love destroy my mother. I remember the moment my mom fell in love for the first time in a long time. After realizing she would never be with my dad, and after discovering he was married, it hurt her, and she has never gotten over it. But amid of it all, our stepdad was horrible in all aspects of our life, and we paid for it dearly. He was the second, and some would say the worst, but nothing beats the third. Nothing!"

"I am sorry, Paris! *I know how much it bothered you to have never met your biological father, but we can always share mine,*" Egypt offers.

"I never met him, and nothing has changed. I'm doing well, and my mother did that herself. As I was saying, I was about ten years old when the third emotional love came into our lives. He was the most damaging of

them all."

"Ah . . . I thought you were going to say he was the one that brought her love back into her life, but I guess I am wrong," Egypt states.

"I believe she wanted to be, but he sent his representative through, and we paid dearly. All of us. My mom was in love for a short time. She wanted to feel real emotional love. The kind that crawls up your back. I wanted it more for her. My mother suffered a lot. He would take her to the movies, hold her hand, and make her feel pretty. I wanted to believe. She was—for a short time, but it ended abruptly. I don't remember my stepfather ever holding my mom's hands or showing any form of affection or love. He was about that physical love. It was painful because it hurt so bad. It's just what we called it, PL. It hurt so bad."

"What happened?"

"You see, he won us over with gifts, kindness, and affection. We were children. We needed what he had to offer. We never really had any type of love shown to us from a man. It was momentary love because one day, he started messing with my sisters and me. At first, I wasn't sure what was happening, and I felt happy that someone liked me or even cared about my siblings and me, but he never really cared at all. That's when the lack of emotional love started to show its face," Paris explains.

"Wait—what?" Egypt says, surprised.

"Yes," Paris continues, "he wasn't a nice person. He was abusive and mean to us all. He abused the girls and tormented the boys and my mom. I always felt guilty for my mother never really knowing what love really was. She never experienced to be a child with her father. It led her down a horrible abusive path. She never knew what it felt to have someone genuinely love her. It's the kind of love that shows up for you, adores you, and never leaves your side. I thought she had finally found it, emotional love, but it destroyed her in the end. I don't think she ever really loved like that again."

"Again, I am sorry for all you and your family went through," Egypt adds.

"Thank you for saying that, but the truth is those old memories will resurface always. She was never the same either. You see, for many years after that, my mom struggled with men, drugs, and alcoholism. She never knew her father, and every other man that came into her life never really cared. She went from man to man, hoping for some form of affection, but it never came. Sometimes I don't think I'll ever find a love that cares for me either."

"Don't say that, Paris," Egypt responds. "Love will find you again."

"I really don't think so. You see, when I was a child, Love taught me never to trust it, and I don't. Love never loved no one, it always took, and it never gave back."

"I am sorry you felt that pain, and you still carry it with you today. You have so much to offer. Know this: I love and will always be here for you," Egypt says.

"I appreciate that, and I love you for it. We have been through a lot, and I appreciate your friendship. This love thang is a crazy unpredictable force. It's the forbidden fruit encompassing emotional Love where treasured waters run deep.

"Paris . . . girl, the man that gets you . . . must know how to relate to you . . . it's not hard, but he needs to put the energy into understanding who you are."

"Maybe I should send them to you so you can tell them that for me. I'm lost when it comes to relating me to men today."

"Absolutely. I got your back always, but before I do, can I get my customary poem?"

"Why, of course, let me leave you with this one for the road. I love you, girl. And thank you for listening."

"Me too, always . . . good night. I know you got something good for me," Egypt responds.

"Yes, sis. This one is called 'Emotional Love' . . . enjoy!"

## EMOTIONAL LOVE

*How does one define Emotional Love?*
*Does it have a picture on it or someone's face?*
*Can I have it all to myself, or do I have to share it?*
*I want to know.*
*When I think about Emotional Love, it feels good.*
*It protects me; it always comforts me. It never leaves me lonely.*
*I wonder about Emotional Love, and sometimes I don't understand it.*
*Love can be so simple and yet complicated, all in one breath.*
*I want to trust Emotional Love; of course, I want to believe in it*
*but how when it has shown me the Emotional Love I desire.*
*Embrace my heart. Fill it with laughter and patience.*
*Help me to know it can happen for me, too.*
*I want this Emotional Love.*
*And never doubt it again. I want limitless possibilities with it.*
*Can I have it? What is everyone's talking about when it has only hurt me?*
*Simply put, I want to feel Emotional Love, with a vengeance!*

# ALL OF YOU

"Hey, girl!" Alanna says as Tameko picks up the phone. "I was just thinking about you—what are you doing Friday night?"

"As far as I know, . . . nothing. Why do you ask, Alanna? The last time you asked me to go out with you, with that guy you tried to set me up with, and you *knew* I wouldn't be attracted to."

"What was wrong with him? He had a job, a career, his apartment."

"Ah, he didn't have no teeth," Tameko yells.

"Ha ha. I'm sorry about that. Why do you sound so suspicious?" Alanna asks.

"You know why I'm suspicious. I have every damn good reason to be."

"Yeah, you're right," Alanna says with a laugh.

"That was *not* funny," Tameko responds, annoyed. "I can deal with a lot . . . but *missing teeth*? Especially in the front? I don't think so."

"Girl, you starting to sound like Paris."

"Just a little funny, funny," Alanna adds.

"I see we got jokes."

"Get to gumming." Alanna chuckles.

"Now what?"

"You know what they say."

"Anyhoo."

"Yeah, what's going on with you?" Alanna asks. "Lately, you've been missing in action. You haven't been hanging out with the girls and me lately! Are you seeing someone? Is there something you don't want us to know about?"

"No, don't be silly. I've just been busy with work and everything."

"If not. What's going on?"

"Maybe I have . . . " Tameko says under her breath.

"Excuse me? Did or did I not just hear you right? Have you? What's that supposed to mean?"

"I thought we should go to the strip club tonight," Tameko says, changing the subject.

"Strip clubs? Really?"

"Yes!"

"Why not? It used to be our favorite thing to do," Tameko adds.

"I thought you didn't like strip clubs, anymore," Alanna says.

"Well, I do now!"

"Remember the last time we went to a strip club? We had to pick Paris's ass up off the floor. She was so drunk, trying to seduce a stripper. We promised never to take her out to a strip club again. That was nearly six months ago."

"I know!" Tameko says, laughing. "But we do the same things repeatedly: restaurants, movies, and clubs. We haven't been there in a while . . . so I thought we could try again."

"I don't want to have to repeat that episode again. Please."

"Okay," Alanna says, "but something doesn't feel right. What's going on? Are you meeting someone there? I never heard you politicking so hard for someone, let alone a place. I assume you have a place in mind too?"

"Yes, as a matter of fact I do," Tameko replies.

"Where?"

"It's called Candy Girls on Fifth."

"Wow, why do I feel like we've been set up? What's really good? Are we meeting here?

"Yes, we are and we're going to have a good time, I promise. Let the girls know we are going to a strip club."

"Stop being suspicious. I just wanted to hang out with the girls for old time's sake. What's wrong with that?"

"Nothing! I guess," Alanna adds

"Look, I don't want to go into this long speech with you. I just want to leave it there. Okay?"

"Okay. But is there going to be guys there?" Alanna asks.

"No disrespect, but that is a stupid question. Of course, there are going to be guys there. It's a strip club. Stop being ridiculous." Tameko's voice rises.

"What's this all about?" Alanna asks, pressing for an answer. "To be honest, you've always been a promiscuous woman, especially when it comes to men. And now you don't want to say who we're meeting?"

"I'd rather not say right now. I'm trying to keep it private."

"Private? How private? No crazy men, right?"

"No, not at all. Damn, what's with the twenty questions," Tameko responds.

"Okay, fine. I'll leave it there for now," Alanna says, giving up.

"Thanks . . . Well, let's give Paris a call, see if she's up for going to the strip club—"

"Wait, before we call Paris. Do you remembered the first time I met that stripper named Panda Bear?" Alanna says, interrupting. "Girl, he was a caramel complexion, tall, dark, and handsome, and the moment he came out on the floor, he had me glued to his every move."

"Yes, I remember. You went into a stance, blacked out, and lost your mind."

"I couldn't contain myself, and I was watching every *inch* of his body. I couldn't take my eyes off him. Girl, I spent nearly $30 on him that night. Just to dance in front of me."

"You went crazy."

"What turned me on about him was he wasn't the arrogant type. He was confident and took his time with me. Tameko, do *you* hear me, girl? He was patient and charming. It felt genuine, he danced just for me. I don't know if I had a little too much to drink or not, but I was in love in that moment—at least until he saw another woman with fifty more singles and left me standing."

Tameko laughs, but Alanna continues.

"I thought I was in love too until the liquor wore off and I was out of my money and had no way to get home. It's funny now, but back then, not at all. "

Tameko falls on the floor laughing. "I remembered that- shit." We had to put all our little monies together to get your ass all the way back to New Jersey.

"And you know Paris. She has a poem for just about every occasion. She gave me a copy. Wait a minute, let me go and get it—I save that shit."

"Dang, you feeling horny, Alanna?" Tameko says with a laugh. "You so damn nasty."

"Maybe I'm just feeling a little lonely," Alanna responds thoughtfully. "Oh! Hold on! I found it. It went like this."

## ALL OF YOU

When I first laid eyes on you, I dripped
With frustration because I could not have you
And I knew it; you were not mine to have.

I could almost feel the stroke of your hand
On my inner thigh, trembling and waiting
Until you extended yourself a little further and deeper!

Damn, you move me in a way I never thought possible!
I'm overwhelmed by your existence, and you never took the time to
Notice me. I just want to take you to that place of
No return, I want to prove to you that I, too, can receive
You in your entirety no matter what you ask of me!

I'm almost at a begging point because I can imagine your
Manhood inside of me; trusting, forcefully, and at the same time
Loving me the way I want to be enjoyed.
Only a man of your caliber can give me exactly what
I totally and completely desire, You!

# UNFORGETTABLE

Tameko continues, "That *was* some deep words to express about someone who was a stripper. I guess we all got a fantasy about someone. Especially if you're not sure if you are going to see them anymore."

"That's the point—you may never know," Alanna responds.

"Yeah, you never know if you're going to see anyone anymore these days. I guess that's why I felt he was staring at my soul capturing my feelings that night. It was unforgettable. I think back to that time we went to the strip club. It was unforgettable. Do you know what I mean?" Tameko recalls.

"No!" Alanna says with a laugh. "I'm not the mushy type. There you go sounding like Paris. She's the only girl I know who expresses words in a way that makes you feel like dang, I wished I wrote them myself."

"Ha ha. Yeah, I know. Well, didn't you say you had a call to make? Go make that call, and I'll call you back later. I need to make some arrangements before my friend comes over this weekend," Tameko states.

"Friend? What new friend you got? I thought we were the only friends you have," Alanna states.

Tameko replies, "You are my sisters, but I do have other friends. I never talk about them to you girls. You ladies get jealous, which turns into territorial."

"No, we're not. What are you talking about? We all have other friends," Alanna states.

"Yes, we do, but we never bring them around each other. I'm done with this conversation, and I got to go. I can't keep *my girl* waiting. We'll talk later."

"Hey . . . hey . . . what? Why are you rushing off?" Alanna states.

"I'm sorry. I just got a lot to do before they and you come over," Tameko adds.

"Did you just say 'my girl'? Is this friend a man or a woman? You *know* how you get down sometimes, Tameko. I'm just saying."

"*I thought* I could introduce my friend to your ladies this weekend, but maybe I was wrong!" Tameko states with an attitude.

"Girl, you're really serious about us meeting your friend, aren't you?"

"Yes, I'm serious about this one. We're close, and I wanted you ladies to get to know her as well. Who knew?"

"Is it a woman or a man? You're confusing me," Alanna says.

"Anyhoo . . . getting back to go to this club thing. Will Panda Bear be there tonight? You know the stripper? I don't mind sitting on his dick tonight," Tameko says playfully.

"No, silly! It's been a long time. I seriously doubt it. The last time we saw him there, it was almost three years ago. Men come and go in the stripping business. It's like changing underwear, putting on a new pair every day," Alanna says with a laugh.

"Yeah, I hear that . . . well, okay then. Go ahead and make plans. Talk to you later!" Tameko clicks off the phone. *Who knows where my heart lies? Unforgettable!* she thinks. *Only God does! It's not easy telling someone your truths. Nonetheless, they must be told. This will be an unforgettable ride.*

## UNFORGETTABLE

*Like the plane in the sky that flies so eloquently*
*It's the same feeling I get when we make love.*
*Never wanting to stop—hold on tight, and don't let go of me!*
*Not a day passes, and you're not embraced with a thought.*
*The languages unspoken, the compass of emotion interacts.*
*Love is so difficult to express, yet I never have to with you.*
*Look what you do to me, loving me the way you do!*
*Explain how our souls lock: comfortably, unselfishly, and*
*Still, I can't claim the very joy within me, like two fools*
*Loving afar. So close, you can feel it, taste it, and understand it.*
*I can—not fair—you're not mine . . . intimately.*
*How can you take it from me? Love me so gracefully, bless me*
*With your presence, only to shun me—I see it in your eyes—*
*Don't look away! Come to me—I'll slow down for you—catch my hand.*
*Say yes, I can!*

# TRYING MY BEST

*Mr. Joh Allen. I've been wondering about him a lot lately,* Paris thinks. *I don't know why. Especially the part where I found him in bed with another woman. Despite the incident, I can't forget what we had and how good it felt with him. We had a fantastic sex life, and the pampering, the conversations were always good too.*

*But then it was over. I admit I didn't handle it well. How could I? I walked in on him in my bed with another woman. After seeing some shit like that, I called him all the names in the book. I have to stop talking to myself like this. In these moments, my mind drifts back to my past with Joh. The moment I walked on him in my bed with another woman. I wanted to kill his ass and hers too. In my house, a home we shared. Who does that? I probably could have handled it better, but then again, why should I. After speaking with my therapist, there was nothing I could have done. I am a woman scorn. I was so hurt. I never imagined in a million years Joh cheating on me. Oh well. All's fair in love and war, I guess. I miss him, though, and I miss him a lot. Girl, you have to stop talking to yourself and answering back too. Ha ha. So what should I do today? I guess I'll treat myself to a day of beauty: the nail salon, a full-body makeover, and a nice bottle of wine . . . not! No, I think I'm just going to stay home, but how I miss making love. I haven't had a good piece of D\*\*K in a while. Ever since Mr. Whatever left, masturbation has become my man with no long-term effects. The feelings wear off too soon, and my thoughts come running back. PTSD is a bit\*\* with no remorse. My fingers aren't enjoyable anymore, and this can't be natural. This isn't fair.*

*Oh well. Let me grab my keys. I have to move my car anyway.*

****

*Wait. My phone is ringing. Of course, shit, it's all the way down at the bottom of my bag. Dang, I missed the call. Whoever it was . . . they'll call back. Wait, I hope it's not who I think it is. Found it, looking at the call log, no, it wasn't. Thank GOD, I met this guy in the supermarket the other day and gave him my number. He has been calling nonstop. Whew, I hope I dodge a bullet, or maybe I am just horny. Surprisingly, it was Mr. Joh Allen, and here he comes toward me! Telepathy, I was thinking about him, and here he is. I guess he was calling to let me know he seen me and wanted to stop by.*

"Hey, Paris," Joh says as he is walking up the street. "How are you doing? How's the family? The ladies? It's been a minute. How're things going with you?"

"All is well, and you? I'm surprised to see you in my neighborhood. What brings you here? How's your family?" Paris asks.

"That's why I am here, to get my family," Joh answers.

"To get your family. I don't understand," Paris states.

"Yes. I came to talk to you."

"What? Why?" Paris is startled.

"Actually . . . wait. I'm sorry. I'm saying too much. I'm just so happy to see you, that's all. You look so good right now. Wait, please don't leave." Joh grabs her hand as Paris starts to turn away.

"Just give me a minute. I need to talk to you," Joh adds.

"I don't think we have anything to talk about, Joh." Paris tries to act casual, but she's caught between wanting to leave—and needing to stay. "What is it that you want, Joh? You got five minutes."

"Is everything's good? The family's doing well. Wow, how long has it been?"

"I think we both said that. Four minutes . . . Joh." Paris smirks.

"Hold on a minute. Can you slow down them minutes? I know, but I am nervous," Joh adds.

"It's been a minute—about two years," Paris says quickly—and then scrambles to change the subject. "I didn't know you still lived in the area, Joh . . . I thought you moved away."

"I did . . . but I came back, my mother has gotten really sick, and she needs my help. So I came back to take care of her."

"I'm not surprised. That's who you are," Paris says, touched. "Well," she continues, resuming her casual tone, "I was on my way to move my car. I don't want to get a ticket. It was nice to see you. Let me not keep you any longer."

"You're not keeping me. I'm so happy to see you. It's been a while, and at this very moment, you are all I want to see. I hope am not being too forward, considering what's happened between us, but . . . I remembered all the good times we had together. As matter of fact . . . that's all I've been thinking about lately."

"I'm surprised. Considering what happened," Paris responds coldly.

"I know. As I said, I'm so sorry about what went down between us. I've had time to think about my part. I should've been stronger, mature, and spoke to my woman, but I made a serious mistake. And it cost me the love of my life," Joh responds.

"You're right," Paris responds. *But after reflecting on it,* she thinks, *I didn't make it easy for you either. I've realized that I shared in that situation too.* "But if you don't mind, I don't want to revisit that moment. It's over, and I have since moved on."

"Oh? *Ah,* I didn't know, but . . . so you've moved on? Well, let me let you go then! It was really good seeing you again, Paris," Joh adds, starting to turn around to leave.

"No . . . I didn't mean . . . I meant I'm trying to move past that moment. It wasn't a good time, and like I said, if I can be upfront."

"Ha ha. You had me nervous. I thought you meant . . . " Joh says.

"No. Not at all," Paris clarifies.

"OH." Joh *realized* what Paris meant.

"Well, it's all good. That was a long time ago. Like I said, let sleeping dogs lie," Paris responds.

"Anyway . . . how are you doing, Paris? I've missed you, honestly. Honestly, I did," Joh states.

"I'm okay, one day at a time," Paris shyly admits.

"Let me just be honest before my time runs out. I haven't been able to get close to anyone, much less a woman. Not since you. It doesn't feel the same. I don't think we had any real closure. Honestly, it always felt like more should've been said between us, but the moment was wrong, and I get that now. I love you as my best friend, and you are the love of my life. You continue to have my whole heart." Joh manages a small smile.

"I am? I do," Paris responds with confidence.

"Absolutely! Can I ask you a question?"

"What?"

"Can I get your number if it's okay with you? I'd like to get to know you again. Can we go to dinner, Paris? Please?"

"It never changed, Joh."

"Thank you *GOD!*" Joh shouts.

Paris can't help but laugh at Joh's burst of enthusiasm. *Little does he know I want him to call me too, and I want my man back too.*

Joh stands directly in front of Paris. "Paris, you still here?" Joh asks, knowing how Paris has the tendency to drift off in thought.

"Yeah . . . I was just thinking about something, but I am fine," Paris states.

"Do you care to share?" Joh asks.

"No, it's okay. If you remember, I do that sometimes," Paris states.

"Oh. Good. I remember, it is one of those rare things I like about you. You are always thinking. I am sure my time is up, and I got to go. I'll call you later if you don't mind."

"I don't mind," Paris belts out.

"I got to get back to my mother. It's time to give her medication. I'm glad we talked."

"Me too," Paris states.

"Thank you, and you won't regret it. I miss you, baby girl, and I promise to treat you better than before."

"Hmmm. Until then. I like the sound of that." Paris smirks. *I really hope I am making a good decision,* Paris thinks as she watches Joh walk away. *But I can't help how I felt when I was with him. I miss this man.*

*No other man has come close to what I felt with him. Today, it becomes a chore to date, instead of enjoyment, no one wants to put in the work to get to know you, let alone invest in you, their time, finances, or concern for your well-being. Not to mention courtship is out of the question. They just want to go straight to the bedroom. Unbelievable!*

*I can almost hear Tameko's voice giving me a lecture: "Girl, do you know how old you are? You better hurry up before you lose your good looks and its covered in grey down there." Always reminding me I am getting older and alone.*

*I guess I can let him take me to dinner and hear what he has to say. Hell, it's been a minute. And if I don't like it, I can leave, but a free meal is always good too. Remember, there comes the point in your relationship when someone may step out—but does it mean that you're stupid to go back? No. It's your relationship. You measure the area of wrongdoing. I'm trying my best . . . to let the past stay where it was and take accountability. I played a part in it too.*

*Here I go again talking to myself and answering also. The decision's totally up to me. I know I'm just trying to convince myself why I shouldn't take this man back, but the truth is, I want him back, and I still love him because I know he loves me!*

*But if it should happen again . . . well, let's just say I'll just have to cut his ding-dong off and feed it to the dogs. Ha ha.*

*Girl, stop talking to yourself. I am always in my thoughts. So, I guess, I'll end this conversation in my head. I'm trying my best. It goes something like this.*

## TRYING MY BEST

*Trying, my best not to feel like a fool again, to be the best version of me*
*My mind plays tricks on me and lets me go back to that place*
*Where we once played, laid, and made plans.*
*You see, my mind tells me to let it go, lets me know that*
*I'm trying my best to forgive me and not relive.*
*Not to take me back to a place where I never saw this happening,*
*it could not be happening because of you and me*
*I'm trying my best to trust this love again, not to*
*fall short of my own need for tranquility.*
*I'm trying my best to say "hello" to <u>me</u> again.*
*Trying my best to remember that*
*girl, lady, and now a woman—that she's trying*
*her best not to go back to being a*
*person who doesn't know her self-worth, understanding*
*her position and recognizing the roles she plays, but*
*most of all she is doing her best not to walk away, but learning*
*how to stay, fight, and be what she wants in all of this*
*Because being respected, staying strong is trying*
*her best to love herself, always!*

# STORY BREAK

# TIME IS CHANGING

*Time is changing*
*And the understanding of life*
*Has been the chances we've learned to take.*
*Moving forward to reach new goals,*
*And learning how to prevail into the future,*
*Has been the challenges we've strived to overcome.*
*Understanding the need to love, and loving the need to*
*Understand.*
*Individuals loathe the obstacles they want to transcend*
*But we must be accepting of life's challenges.*
*What does this all mean? Is it the experience expressed in words?*
*That escalate and develop into the mind of the prevailing word, called*
*Change?*
*Here, I've come to give the full understanding of change,*
*With the knowledge*
*That change is a matter of acceptance of what will be*
*And how it will grow and become what I know—only to arrive*
*To what I have become. Time is changing, and*
*the changing of time has captured*
*The fiber of me!*

# LOVE TAUGHT BY YOU

"Hey, Joh. What's going on, man?" Ian answers, surprised. "It's been a minute since we've seen or talked to each other, brother. Hey, how're those Yankees doing?"

"They all right. You know I am a Giants fan. Maybe we will have a subway series soon," Joh replies.

"Yeah . . . well, maybe. To what do I owe the pleasure of your call?" Ian chuckles.

"Just reaching out to my brother. Can I do that? I thought maybe we could meet up for drinks. I have something I want to talk to you about," Joh states.

"Okay, sounds great. How's tonight? Egypt will be out with the kids, and I usually go out to shoot some pool."

"Tonight sounds good. See you then. At the same spot, I presume."

"Yeah, the same spot on Fifth," Ian answers.

*"Okay, great, see you then," Joh says.*

*I wonder what Joh has to talk with me about,* he thinks. *It's been two years since his breakup with Paris. We haven't spoken since, but it felt like yesterday. Shit happens. I hope it's not about him and Paris. I promised Egypt I would stay out of it. But what if he asks? Then what am I going to do? I hate drama, especially when it involves women—but this is my boy.*

\*\*\*

*It must be dire if Joh wants to talk to me,* Ian thinks as he gets ready to go out. *We've never really gotten into the personal talk before. I mean, men rarely talk about their own stuff. It's just not our style. We find it corny, but truth be told, we need to talk more about personal issues. By talking, we learn how to be better fathers, sons, brothers, husbands, and leaders in our families and to ourselves.*

"Ian?" Egypt yells from the front room. She must've returned with the kids. "Are you still here?"

"Yes, but I'm about to go out," Ian yells back.

"Okay! Babe, can you pick up some muffins and jelly on your way back?"

"Sure, but it'll be a while. I'm going to catch up with Joh."

"What? When did y'all start hanging out again?" Egypt asks as she comes into the room.

"I admit it's been a minute, but he just called and asked if we can get together." "He's my man. I'mma always going to be there for him, even if we don't speak for a while."

"Okay, just asking. As I was saying, can you pick up some muffins and jelly for Sunday's breakfast?"

"Sunday breakfast? Bae, I didn't know we were having breakfast."

"Yes, babe, I told you last week," Egypt replies.

"Oh! That conversation! When we're engaging in all that pillow talk?"

Ian smiles. "Right, that pillow talk. Ha ha."

*Yessss . . . that conversation!* Egypt smiles back.

*See how easily a man forgets,* Egypt thinks. "It's okay. I'll see you later . . . "

\*\*\*

As Ian walks into the restaurant, he sees the relief on Joh's face.

"Hey, Ian. I thought you weren't going to make it," his friend says.

"Why would you think that? I told you I would come," Ian replies.

"I just needed someone to talk to. Are we still good?" Joh asks.

"What's up?" Ian replies.

"I apologize, it's been a minute, but I had to get my head together, youknowwhatImean?" Joh responds.

"Yes, I do. Okay, shoot," Ian replies.

"Well, if you didn't know, I cheated on Paris the last time we were together. It was a long time ago. We recently ran into each other, and after realizing how much we missed each other, we got to talking and decided to try it again."

"I'm sorry, try what?" Ian asked.

"Working on our relationship. It took a long time for her to forgive me, but she did," Joh states.

"And?" Ian replies.

"I learned my lesson. Honestly, I was just greedy," Joh says.

"Okay, I'm listening. So, what's the problem? Make it clear, brother."

"The problem is, I have this secretary, and she's starting to get to me. I can feel it. I don't want to cheat on Paris, but this secretary of mine . . . *wow*. I'm about to—"

"You about to *what*?" Ian interrupts. "Cheat? You didn't call me down here so I can cosign to your bullshit? Wasn't cheating once enough? You didn't cheat once but now twice, and you ain't even good at it." Ian's voice rises.

"No, not at all. But I really want to though. I think about it, but I'm not stupid. Did I tell you how gorgeous she is?" Joh states.

"Brother, you're thinking about this too long. Do you need a reminder of how bad your breakup was, how bad Paris was hurt, and how much praying and forgiveness you needed? Do you . . . naw, brother. You don't need a rewind."

"You're right! I was just thinking. I'm just kidding. Ha ha."

"Funny, I don't think you know. I don't think you know just how bad it was, or you wouldn't be asking me about this crap," Ian states.

"I know, brother. That's why you're here! Honestly," Joh says, "ah, ah, I don't have any plans on cheating on Paris again. I know the depth of pain I caused."

"Okay . . . so you got jokes. Laughing my ass. Why?"

"Greed, I guess. Opportunity! I realized that now!" Joh states.

"I don't know what your problem is, but you need to grow up," Ian says.

Honestly, I just never thought I would get caught," Joh responds.

"I've heard that before. Most guys don't. How's that going for you?" Ian asks.

"It's better. We've been communicating, working on our relationship. I know I want to marry this woman. I admit I'm nervous she hasn't fully forgiven me and won't want to marry me," Joh replies.

"Wait. When did we get to marriage?" Ian asks.

"The moment I laid eyes on her. I may joke about cheating. I have no intentions of cheating on Paris again. I want to marry her."

"Honestly, you may want to think about getting some relationship counseling," Ian states.

"Counseling . . . we're not even married yet," Joh answers.

"No, you're not. Today, you can do premarital counseling before getting married. It's known to work, and it can't but help," Ian states.

"I think that might be a great idea. I'm going to talk to Paris and see if she is willing to do it."

"If I know Paris . . . she'll be willing," Ian states.

"Really, it seems like you have the perfect relationship with Egypt," Joh states.

"Yes, I do. You know, even though Egypt and I have been together, we've been to counseling to maintain our marriage. Nothing is perfect."

"Does it help?" Joh asks.

"Yeah, well, to keep it going, we get the help we need. No matter what happens after that, go to the table and sit down, talk about what you guys are expecting from each other. This way, you'll get better at an understanding of what's expected from each other. Set up boundaries. Egypt and I always go to the table not just when things are wrong but also when they're right," Ian states.

"I understand," Joh replies.

"But whatever you do . . . don't cheat. It never helps anything. It only causes more discord. It's not the answer, and it won't solve anything. Didn't you say you were working things out?" Ian asks.

"Yes, but women's *thoughts.* They never forget."

"Would you forget . . . if she cheated on you?"

"Of course not. But she wouldn't cheat."

"Would you forgive her?" Ian asks again.

"Nope. No! I wouldn't. Call it being chauvinistic," Joh states.

"You wouldn't take her back?" Ian replies. "See? We expect them to take us back, but admittedly we would never take them back.

"Call it what you will. Egypt got you whipped . . . you sound like a straight wimp right now!"

"Unfortunately, it's the truth. We want them to forgive us, get over it, and move on within two days as if nothing happened," Ian states.

"You got that right," Joh replies.

"You see, that's what I mean. Do you even realize how immature you sound? You cheated on her. Now, you want all this in your time—not hers! Knowing if it were her, you wouldn't think about giving her another chance." Ian's voice rises.

"You're right. I wouldn't dare taker her back. That's tainted. Call it being a man . . . but many brothers would agree with me!" Joh answers.

"Okay then. Let's end this conversation," Ian states.

"I think we should," Joh responds.

"If you're really serious about asking her to marry you, first, you've got to grow up and take this shit seriously," Ian says.

"I am. More than you know," Joh replies.

"How and when were you planning to pop the question?"

"On Sunday at breakfast."

"Breakfast? What breakfast and where?" Ian's voice rises.

"Your house. You do know about the breakfast were having at your house? I asked your wife to set it up for me. I hope you don't mind," Joh states.

"Why would I mind? We're family. Mind! Here I am thinking it's about something else. No, I don't care. I just didn't know about it." Ian sulks.

"Hey, are you sure you're okay with it? Sunday breakfast?"

"Nothing. You wouldn't understand," Ian says, sulking under his breath. "How come I'm the last to know?"

"Because you don't know how to keep a secret. You got a big mouth," Joh states under his breath.

"Did you say something?" Ian asks.

"Nope," Joh replies.

"So what time is this breakfast? How many people are you expecting to come?" Ian asks.

"About twenty-five people. We should be starting around 10:00 a.m. Is that okay? Are you sure you okay? Honestly, I thought Egypt talked this over with you. I am sorry if I . . . "

"10:00 a.m. is more like brunch, not breakfast," Ian replies.

"Brunch or breakfast, it doesn't matter as long as she says yes," Jon states.

"Great, I am glad for you and Paris. Don't mess this up, Joh. It's all good."

"I spent the last two years without her. I'm not about to spend any more time without her. I never felt settled or relaxed since she left. I felt alone, disoriented . . . we were so close, and I messed it up," Joh states.

"Mistakes happened. Look, twenty-five people are a lot of people in my house. Make sure you watch . . . I don't know them."

"Okay . . . if anything happens, breaks, I'll pay for it. No worries," Joh states.

"Anyway . . . getting back to you and Paris . . . . you got to forgive yourself because it looks like Paris almost has. Don't live in the past . . . there's no room for it," Ian states.

"I know, man. I'll get over it the moment she says yes!" Joh answers.

"Then let's get this girl to the altar." Ian laughs.

"When I think about my childhood, being raised in a single-parent household, I didn't understand how hard it was until now. I loved and respected my mother, but I gave her hell as a child. I was angry for a long time. I was not being raised by my father, him leaving us early on, and leaving my mother to raise us alone. It made me bitter for a long time," Joh recalls.

"I'm sorry, I didn't know that about you. I get it, but that wasn't your fault or your mother's. It was his choice," Ian replies.

"I know that now, but I blamed her for a long time."

"It caused me to be less emotionally connected to women until Paris came along."

"I can relate. Why now?" Ian asks.

"Because one day he was there, and the next he was gone. My mother never talked about it, and so I grew up thinking she ran him away," Joh states.

"And now?" Ian replies.

"Some years down the road, my father returned, and I was still so outraged, and he told me it wasn't Mom's fault. It was his. He felt it was too much for him, and he left. He admitted he abused her, and he cheated."

"Did he tell you all of that? Maybe this explains your behavior toward women," Ian states.

"Yes. Call it guilt or something. He's getting sick, and my mother is his beneficiary to all his business. He still trusts her and wants her to take care of the stuff if something should happen to him."

"Wow. Man! I didn't know, but I am glad he came back and admitted his mistakes. That takes a big man to do that," Ian answers.

"Honestly, at first I was mad, but I got over it. I am a grown man, and I don't have to commit the same mistakes he did, but I am glad he told my siblings and me the truth. I'm sure it wasn't easy," Joh states.

"But he did," Ian states.

"What I've learned is misery loves company, and it will find you. I'm not going back to that dark place. When you know better, you do better! We all have a responsibility toward one another," Joh states.

"I know that now," Ian responds. "And every day I work toward being my brother's keeper."

"All I know is my life isn't anything without Paris—and I'll spend the rest of my life proving it to her. I felt lost for a while. And I never want to feel that feeling again, never! How do you do it, Ian?"

"It takes a lot of work and dedication," Ian admits, "and of course, commitment. When you're ready, you give unselfishly. If you don't think you're ready, be a grown-up about it and back out. It's better to say, 'I'm not ready,' than to lie and hurt the people you claim to love."

"I get it, Ian. I really do," Joh says.

"Men . . . we not built for this emotional stuff. We're physical beings, but when you love, your souls interlock and become one entity. It's only then that you'll understand the true essence of sacrificing yourself for somebody else," Ian states.

"I get it, got it, done!" Joh responds. "Paris won't have to worry about her this man cheating again. I *do* understand. It took a minute, but I'm on task and ready to be a better man for myself and her."

"Enough said. Well, I only hope that Ms. Paris—or should I say, Mrs. Paris Tomay—forgives too." Ian says thoughtfully. "The names sound good together."

"They do. I've been practicing the proposal for a minute now, in the shower, out loud. I am nervous as hell. I am praying for a good response."

"It will go well. You got this," Ian says with confidence.

"Mrs. Paris Tomay! I love the way that sounds."

"Speaking of the proposal," Ian continues, "did you decide how you want the day to flow?"

"Yes!" Joh answers. "Egypt and I have been working on this for about three months."

"Three months! And where was I when all this planning was going on?"

"I'm not sure. I thought Egypt would have told you, brother, and I hope it's all good now, right?"

"It's all good," Ian says hesitantly.

"Well, okay then," Joh continues. "We'll meet at your house at about 10:00 a.m. Greetings will begin, and then, as we sit down for breakfast, at approximately ten-thirty, the first set of roses will arrive at the house—anonymously."

"Anonymously?" Ian replies.

"Yes, it's all a part of the surprise," Joh answers.

"Wow. You guys have been planning this for a while, I see."

"Yeah, we have," Joh says. "I wanted it to be special, and with the people we love. Egypt has been helpful. She understood I want my girl back. And then around 11:00 a.m., another set of roses and a small box of chocolates will arrive. And then, at about eleven-thirty—another set of roses!"

"Another set of roses. After all this, I'm going to have to go out and buy my wife two dozen roses, and maybe a necklace or something. Otherwise, I'll be in the doghouse for a very long time," Ian says with a laugh.

"I told you, I have a lot of making up to do," Joh replies.

"I see you do. That girl is going to bankrupt your ass." Ian laughs again.

"And then," Joh continues, "in the final hour, another box of roses will come, and in the last box, it'll have a diamond ring. And then I'm going to sing to her."

"Sing? Seriously? All of this is going on in my house. You're making me look bad in front of my wife! I'm scared to ask . . . what's the name of the song?"

"It's Kenny Lattimore's 'Love Will Find a Way.' From *The Lion King,*" Joh answers.

"That's a hot song, man!" Ian states excitedly.

"Yeah, it is. When we went to the play, Paris loved that song. I thought it fit the moment," Joh answers.

"Well, I'm happy for you," Ian responds. "You sure this is what you want?"

"No question, Ian! I love that woman!"

"Life's too short to spend another minute alone," Ian says as the men head toward the door. "Wow . . . look at what love has taught you. Like Morgan Freeman once said, you either get busy living or get busy dying. 'Cause, in the end, we can't take anything with us except our memories, and even then—how much of it have we paid attention to?"

"Thanks, brother, for coming out with me. I started writing poetry again. I have a poem for this occasion. It's called 'Love Taught by You'!"

"Damn, Paris is good . . . *she got you* writing poetry. Ha ha," Ian states.

## LOVE TAUGHT BY YOU

*When I look into your eyes*
*I see my dreams, my desires,*
*And all I want to be.*
*I open my heart to yours*
*And you showed me how to take things slowly*
*You showed me how to be patient*
*You taught me how to love. And I thank you!*
*Trust is something I never knew.*
*It was only an imaginary feeling*
*To never be expanded upon.*
*But now, when I think about Love, it's you!*
*You make all the difference to me*
*And I never had a chance to tell you,*
*But now I do! Lover of my soul!*
*My destiny waits to see all that I will*
*Accomplish through and with you!*

*I'll wait; it's just a matter of time.*
*Take me, do what you will.*
*I don't have to worry or think about what*
*This brings*
*Because it has already arrived!*
*Patience brings the best of everything.*
*What I desire most*
*Is loving you to a capacity that most would call a*
*Rarity! Love taught by you.*

# MEMORIES

"Hello, hello?"

*Dang, someone just keeps calling and hanging up. There it goes again!* Paris thinks to herself. *Maybe it's Massai. If it is him, I wish he'd stop because I'm not going back to him. Especially since Joh and I are so close to reconciling.*

"Hello, hello," Ian says. He is trying to call Paris, but the phone drops and makes it hard to connect.

*And here it goes again! Whoever this is, I'm going curse them out. This shit is getting on my nerves, and not to mention it's a little scary. Ever since I made district attorney, I've been receiving some crank calls.*

"Hello? Who is this?" Paris answers. "Stop calling my damn house!"

"Hello? Paris? It's me, Ian!"

"Ian? Was that you who just called? I thought I heard someone saying hello, but I couldn't make out your voice. But, oh, hey, Ian!" Paris feels relieved it isn't another crank call. *But why in the hell is Ian calling me for? Is everything all right?* "Are Egypt and the kids okay?"

"Yes," Ian responds. "They're beautiful. I just wanted to talk to you, and you're okay? I'm just going to get to the point. Honestly, I don't know where to begin. Let me start with, I know you and Egypt are good friends."

"Yeah. And?"

"The reason I called is I needed to get some advice from a person she respects and knows her well," Ian says in a hurry.

"What's on your mind, Ian?" Paris answers, still not understanding the purpose of his call.

"I guess I'm just a little nervous coming to you. Excuse me," Ian replies.

"About what? You're beating around the bush again, Ian."

"Okay, here it is. I think Egypt is having an affair."

"What? What do you mean an affair? Why would you think that? Has she given you a reason?" Paris almost fell off her seat; she couldn't believe what she was hearing. *That girl better not be having an affair. Did we just have this conversation?* "Why would you think that?" Paris asks again.

"I don't know . . . something is off," Ian replies.

"What do you mean off?"

"I don't know," Ian responds.

"You keep saying that, but you need to be sure. Has any of her routines changed? Or admitted to anything?"

"No . . . and . . . yes."

"You need to be clear about this shit really quick, Ian. What is the no, and what is yes?"

"Yes, her routine has changed a lot lately. And she is not admitting to anything. I guess I am just worried, that's why I'm calling," Ian replies.

*I don't understand,* Paris thinks. "When we last talked, everything seemed fine. I haven't talk to her lately. What's changed?"

"She has been coming in late lately. She was late at least three times last week, and she never wants to talk anymore. She's always on the phone whispering, and she won't tell me who she's talking to. I feel kind of embarrassed talking to you about it. You're her best friend. Maybe we shouldn't be having this conversation," Ian says, second-guessing his decision to call Paris. "I'll talk to you later."

"No . . . no . . . *don't hang up!* We can talk right now. And I promise that whatever we discuss stays between you and me, Ian," Paris states.

"Okay . . . I still feel funny," Ian hesitantly replies.

"So . . . getting back to the issue at hand, maybe she's tired, Ian."

"Has she talked to you about us, Paris?" Ian asks, nervous at what the answer will be.

"No, she hasn't." *I couldn't tell Ian. Egypt and I already had this conversation, and I thought I got her straight on some things,* Paris thinks. "Ian, are you still there?"

"Yes, I am. Did she say anything to you? Sorry to bring you into the middle of this."

"Honestly, we've talked, but nothing about she wasn't happy or anything like that. I wish I could tell you more. I can give her a call if you like."

"No! I don't want her to think I don't trust her or anything like that," Ian states. "Let me again apologize for calling. I'm just worried. I'm getting antsy and anxious, and I don't know what to do."

"I think you might need to sit Egypt down and let her know how you're feeling," Paris exclaims.

"Lately . . . it just seems her mind is elsewhere. And we're not getting anywhere lately. I don't know what she is thinking. I don't want to lose her and my family, but the sad thing is I don't know if it's me or if it's not."

"Well, I doubt that very much," Paris reassures him. "Egypt loves you and your family." *And if she is having an affair,* she thinks, *I'm going to kill her when I get my hands on her.*

"I know she does, Paris. But maybe LOVE is not enough anymore."

"Well, honestly, I don't have the answers. I know one thing you need to speak with your wife. Is your sex life okay? Whoops, I am sorry. Sometimes my mouth gets the best of me."

"I am okay with it. Your family and I need answers."

"Well, not the missionary position, either. I hope you don't mind me being too personal, Ian, but I need to ask your questions, objectively."

"I'm okay. We're okay in that area. I called you, Paris!"

"Maybe the routine has gotten boring. The children are getting older, and maybe it's time to take the relationship to a different level."

"I need to figure some things out," Ian states.

"You guys were so young when you got married. Maybe you should be thinking of ways to get the romance back into your marriage.

Perhaps a weekend getaway or doing something just for the two of you. Sometimes they help because you can use that time to talk with no interruptions. I'll watch those two monsters of yours. They need to spend time with their godmommy anyway," Paris adds.

"Maybe you're right, Paris. I need to spice up the love life just a little."

"Not a little—a lot," Paris mutters.

"Excuse me . . . has Egypt talked to you . . . you seemed very strong in your opinions." Ian notices.

"Ah . . . ah . . . not at all. Did I say that . . . do not mind me," Paris replies.

"Okay . . . thank you for letting me talk to you. It was great," Ian states reluctantly.

"Hey, before you go, putting in work is a part of the job. Sometimes regression plays a big role in failing relationships and marriages. A relationship doesn't just take communication—you have to learn how to wear many hats, and when dealing with women, it takes several."

"I know what you mean," Ian replies with a laugh.

"Why are you laughing, Ian?" Paris asks.

"Men need to learn how to communicate better in all their relationships, especially women. We do sometimes take it for granted." Ian states. "I'm working on changing that conversation."

Paris pauses a moment and then responds, "I *do* understand how you feel, Ian, and I only hope you continue to work at it. *Fortunately, we women, we don't have that—problems expressing ourselves. We're good at communicating with each other, but we can be vicious toward each other and vindictive. We are our worst enemies.*"

"Thanks, Paris. It's been straightforward talking to you. Please don't tell Egypt we had this discussion . . . she'll never forgive me. She's very private, and I don't want her to know I came to her friends for advice. She won't understand," Ian states.

"She won't. Besides, I don't want you—only she does," Paris jokes. "But seriously, I promise I won't. Just do what I said and if that doesn't work, let me know so I can straighten her ass right out. Remember what I said: stay consistent."

\*\*\*

*That conversation with Paris was intense,* Ian thinks as he puts a vase of flowers on the dinner table. *And it opened my eyes to how lazy I've been with my wife—I've been taking her for granted, not spending quality alone time with her. Realizing my mistake now, but there are so many couples who can't see the forest for the trees and end up losing everything they once had.*

*Is that . . . ?* Ian thinks, hearing keys jangle. He walks to the front door. "Hey, baby, how was your day?"

"It was okay, Ian." She attempts to walk past him. "Why are you in such a good mood?"

"I have a surprise for my baby girl." *After that conversation with Paris, why waste any more time?* Ian thinks. *There's nothing like the present, so let's get started.*

"What?" Egypt asks, surprised. Ian may be romantic, but he had always lacked a certain spontaneity.

"Just close your eyes and take my hand," he continues, purring in her ear. "Baby, it's all about you tonight. Just drop everything at the front door, and I mean everything."

"Even my clothes, shoes, bags, everything! Where are the kids?" Egypt asks, concerned.

"They're with Paris. And yes, I meant everything. I've already run a bath for you."

"Where are we going, and what smells so good?"

"Well, if you must know, I cooked dinner. Or should I say—I had dinner prepared for the two of us. But right now, I need you to go and get into the bath I prepared for *you*," Ian says with a smile.

"Did, you prepare all this for me?"

"Yes, I did—all for you."

"Ian, what's going on?"

"Let me do this for you!" Ian interjects before Egypt can ask any more questions. "I just wanted to do something nice for you."

Egypt is in awe. This isn't like Ian. But she must admit she loves the new Ian. "I hope this isn't a one-time show. Biatch will be mad. I'm just saying. Okay, babe, I'm getting into the bath now!" *Dang, it's been a long time since Ian did anything like this for me,* she thinks. *But knowing him, it won't last long. But I wished he would romance me more often. Maybe it had to do with Paris's engagement party I am planning.*

***

"Egypt, are you almost finished?" Ian calls from outside the bathroom door.

"Yes! Just about, babe!" she answers.

"Come into the bedroom. I laid out something for you."

"Evening wear? Are we going somewhere, Ian?"

"Yes. You'll see," Ian answers.

Egypt moves a little quicker, wondering what had gotten into him. *I like it though,* she thinks.

"Egypt, are you ready?"

"Yes. But really—what's going on?" Egypt's curiosity increases by the second. *What's going on? Who is this new Ian?* "For the last three months, I missed you, and you were busy, and I was beginning to think other thoughts."

"What thoughts?" Ian asks.

"I don't want to get into that right now," Egypt states.

"Okay. It can wait," Ian answers.

*I wonder what Ian is thinking. I hope he doesn't know about the party for Joh and Paris. Ian doesn't know how to keep a secret.*

"You know, woman, you ask too many questions. Close your eyes and come with me . . . are you ready?" Guiding her down the stairs, he whispers, "Open your eyes . . . surprise!"

"It's a real waiter, serving us a full-course meal? He is right here in the middle of our living room. Is this for real, bae? Champagne, pasta, and strawberry cheese tarts . . . all my favorites." Egypt sighs appreciatively. *And if the waiter cleans up after,* Egypt thinks, *well, that would be the cherry on top of a beautiful evening.*

Egypt watches Ian as he talks to the waiter. He slips him something.

"Everything is all taken care of: cleaning and all," states Ian.

"What? Really? You mean I don't have to do the dishes, clean up, nothing?" Egypt asks.

"No. It's all taken care of, baby, just relax."

*Who are you? What did you do with my husband?* Egypt laughs.

"Egypt?" Ian asks, interrupting her train of thought.

"Ah . . . ah, yes, babe. I was just thinking how surprised I am, and how much I could get used to this."

"I want you to get used to this . . . was there something else? It seemed as though you were thinking for a long time, woman."

"Oh, yes! How much I love you too, man!" But as the waiter served the salad, she again thinks, *Oh my God. He can't change like that almost overnight. Wait, Paris. Ian must've talked with her. I know my girl. She told it like it was. No . . . he wouldn't do that. He's too private. Well, anyway, does it doesn't matter. I got my old man back, and I'm loving this already.*

"Egypt, there you go again—in a world of your own," Ian states.

"No, Ian, I was just thinking about how lucky I am to have a man who cares enough about me . . . to go through all this for me."

"Egypt, baby, I would do this a thousand times if I could keep that smile on your face. I gotta say, I was nervous—you stopped looking at me with those starry eyes, and I became a little scared of losing my favorite girl."

"Oh. I see. So this is all because you thought that I had eyes for another man? And you became jealous?"

"No. Not at all. Well, maybe I was just a little concerned because I realized I wasn't keeping my end of the bargain. Remember, I promised to always treat you like the day we first met."

"Yes, and I promised to have homecooked meals, wear a negligee occasionally. Where did we go wrong, Ian, baby? Where?"

"We both became complacent with life, Egypt, and we forgot the most important people: us! But from this day forward, I'll strive harder to live up to my end of the bargain."

"I will too, baby. It's not about me all of the time."

"Really. Say that again. I couldn't hear you." Ian shares a laugh.

"Okay. I got it. I have been selfish. But dang," Egypt says, changing the subject. "This food looks good. Let me see what we have here? Lobster, fettuccini alfredo with shrimp, spinach in butter sauce. Oh my! And the best champagne money can buy! You really went out on a limb for this, Mr. Man."

"Yes, only the best for my girl."

"Do you have any dessert?" Egypt says with a smile.

"You're so greedy, Egypt."

"Well! You can't have all this food and no dessert!"

"I thought I would save the best for last . . . me!"

"Does that 'me' come with strawberry cheese tarts?" She asks cheekily.

He responds in the same tone. "Only if you want it to."

"I do . . . mmm mmm!"

Egypt turns around and sees a strawberry tart from her favorite bakery across town. She gasps.

"Man! You want some of that stuffing and sauce tonight?"

"I better get some stuffing and sauce tonight, no question!" Ian says mischievously.

Egypt lets her thoughts run wild. Again. *I want you to slide that tongue down my back as I lean across the table and gently take your hand to stroke my inner thigh.*

*"I think we may have to leave the rest of this meal, babe. Let's go!"*

Egypt can hear herself purring. *"I think about the memories of what we once shared. I remember it all too well. My mouth is moist just from the anxiety of waiting so long to feel what I once forgot felt so good. Damn, I do remember the champagne baths, the watercolor lovemaking, and I can taste it too. If only you knew what was on my mind at this very moment."*

"I don't have to know. I can see it. Those eyes always let me know what time it is. It's time for watercolor lovemaking. I got you."

"Yes. You do. Do you know what else I'm thinking?"

"Yeah, I do. We should skip dessert. Or add it to the bedroom menu." he says with a smile.

"That's it. Ah, ah. After all, strawberry cheese tarts go well with personal whipped cream . . . Memories are a beautiful thing when two people share in the same moment of thought."

# MEMORIES

*What can we give to one another that we haven't already given?*
*More time, more love, more understanding.*
*It felt like we had all these things!*
*When I look through the hourglass*
*Of our love, the bottom seems endless.*
*But something tells me that time can't*
*Wait us forever.*
*So I just want to*
*Hold on to the memories of yesterday.*
*I don't want to move further away,*
*And risk the changing of time captured.*
*I would give anything to go back to that*
*Time, place, of watercolor love, blissful kisses,*
*And bountiful promises made just for me.*

*Being with you has been a picture-perfect romance for me:*
*Beds of roses, champagne baths, and moonlight massages of music.*
*Embellishing the thought of love inside of me within the depths of your*
*long fingers. It has been endless sessions of slow dancing—sweet memories*
*You and I are loving each other!*

# SHE SAID

*Every time I consider the changes that we put women go through,* Joh thinks, *I can honestly say we do a lot, and rarely do we take responsibility for our actions. Getting caught is never our real issue. We just want you to take us back without any questions. Selfish, I know, but it is just how men are. As long we don't get caught, it never happened. Cheating is not the answer, but maybe we should take a closer look at ourselves. It's not always okay to expect our women to forgive us. We know we wouldn't share the same thought. Your ass is out on the curb quicker than picking up your bag. It's over! Maybe it's time "we men" spend more time talking about real issues instead of just kickin' it and shooting pool. Let me start by getting the brothers together. I think I'll start by calling Ian.*

"Hey, Ian. It's me, Joh."

"Yeah, what's up, man?"

"I thought maybe we could get the brothers together and do some male bonding."

"Male bonding?" Ian asks.

"Shoot some pool, talk and stuff. Just kickin' it."

"Um, I wanted to say thank you again. The breakfast was beautiful, and you and Egypt did your thing."

"Yeah, for a minute, I wasn't sure what was going on with all the whispering and stuff, but it looks like it all came together."

"Sorry about that. *Man,* I really wanted to tell you, but . . . you know!"

They handclap.

Ian replies, "Yeah . . . I know. I can't keep a secret. Ha ha! Anyway, I am really glad you guys worked things out because we all aspire to have what you two have. Black love is important."

"I know what you mean . . . speaking of black love, how about you, the brothers, and I get together?" Joh states.

"You know what, that's a good idea. Let me call Brian, and maybe Massai. I heard Massai is doing much better this time around, and we should show him support," Ian states.

"You're right. Massai *is* trying to get it together this time," Joh replies. "I saw him the other day, and we talked for a while."

"What day are you talking about? You know I gotta square it with Egypt," Ian says.

"Is this weekend good provided everyone's free?" Joh asks.

"I think we good. I'll get back to you on that," Ian replies.

"I'm out." Joh hangs up.

Ian hangs up the phone and places it on the bedside table. *Let me roll over onto this warm, vibrant body of my wife's and self-indulge for a little while longer. She's again becoming my friend and lover-of-life, and our lovemaking has not faltered on any level—and I genuinely enjoy that.*

"Mm mm . . . " Egypt murmurs sleepily. "What are you doing, man?"

"I'm making myself comfortable with *my* body," he says as Egypt begins to purr. "It's been a long time."

"Yes, I know. What a couple of hours. You gotta give a man a chance to reup."

"I'm sorry, babe," Egypt says lovingly.

"I am ready to fillet this cat, now, while you taste this filet mignon," Ian responds.

"Awww, awww, I never forgot how good that felt," Egypt applauds.

"Thank you for never giving me a reason to wonder what, when, and how we got to where we are today. From the moment we met, I've never regretted loving you. And I'll work twice as hard to make sure you never forget it, too."

Egypt looks up and notices Ian looking at her too. She replies, "I know you will, baby, and so will I. We are in this together. That's why I'm so glad we decided to spend more time loving on each other. And the fact you can still tell me a joke or two—as if we just met. And I still laugh! I love you for that. But wait. Maybe I'm just dreaming, but weren't you just talking to the fellas on the phone?"

"Only because you dozed off for a moment. We're going to get together this weekend, shoot some pool, and just kick it."

"You know—Massai is home," Egypt says suddenly.

"Yeah, I know. Paris told me."

"Yes, well, he's doing well this time, and I thought we could all get together sometimes and just bring each other up to speed. You know what we're trying to do, individually and collectively."

"That's a good idea." Ian nods. "Is Paris ready for that?"

I believe she is . . . especially since she and Joh are working things out. It's all behind her, and according to Paris, she and Massai always shared a good friendship. Not to mention, I think Massai is seeing someone too."

"Oh really! He never mentioned it," Ian responds, surprised.

"Yeah, I believe he is. No one has seen her yet. So maybe this will be a great time to meet her."

"Okay. One of the things I want to do is explore how we can give back to the community."

"Are you serious, Ian?"

"Yes, babe!"

"Like what, a community center?" Egypt asks.

"Something like that, but I'm not sure yet. I thought it was one of the things that we fellas could discuss this weekend."

"I think that'll be a good idea. *In the meantime, can we get back to our time? I think something is about purr again.*"

*"Absolutely, where are my manners? Where was I?"*

*The two continue their deep and romantic lovemaking while intensifying every part of one another's bodies. They've come to appreciate the joy of loving to the capacity that most couples only hope to reach.*

***

As Ian walks in, he states, "I don't think you guys know just how important you are to me . . . I just left my lady at home in bed."

"We get it, and so did I," Massai yells across the room as he walks over to meet Ian at the door.

"So, what is going on with y'all?" Ian waves to Joh. "Is that Brian?" He notices Brian walking his way. "Yo, what's up? I have not seen you in a minute," Ian states.

"I know, but I am good. Thank you for including me in this," Brian states.

"Well, ummm, Ian . . . " Massai says as he walks back from the bar with some drinks over to the table. "What is this about?"

"Hey Brah,. . .you good? Massai!" Brian asks.

"Not really! Being that I haven't been home for a long while—and I'm desperately trying to put myself back together—I need some help from you brothers. Remember, when we said we would always be our brother's keeper?"

"Yeah, Massai, I did . . . but . . . " Brian answers this time. The others haven't seen Brian in a while. Not since the incident with Alanna—and her sister.

"Well, when I was up north, what happened to the brotherhood?" Massai says. "You guys just left me hanging, and I haven't heard from nonna y'all. I thought you would always stand by me."

"We did, and I have," Brian answers. "But this time, baby boy, you needed to learn tuff love. Throughout our childhood, I've always been your right hand—but you kept doing the same things. You needed to be in the streets, and it didn't help you've always been selfish. This time I've decided to leave well-enough alone and let you live. Don't forget—I did time, too. And *you* never came to see me. But I let that go. But when you came home this last time, you started smelling your ass, and I knew it was a matter of time before you go back."

"I did, didn't I? Ha ha," Massai admits.

"Yeah. And back you went. I realized you can't help someone who's not ready to be helped."

"Well, Brian, my man . . . thanks for your tuff love," Massai says. "Even though I don't always like the way you lay it on me. But this time I got it. Changing the topic, how have you guys been, and what you been up since I been gone? How's the family doing, Ian?"

"All is well. Egypt and I are still together and doing much better. It was touch and go for a minute, but we worked it out," Ian replies.

"That's good to hear," Massai responds.

"As for Alanna and me . . . I really messed that up," Brian answers.

"We know," Joh says.

"Her sister, bro?" Ian states.

"By the time I paid attention, I realized, I was stupid. I mess up a good thing. Now Alanna is gone. As for her sister, I should have never gone there. I was just being stupid.

We've all been there. Ian responds

Hell, I remember the 'he said, she said' conversations we all used to have, sharing our dreams and desires in life," Massai follows.

"Well, my man," Brian says, "the past is over, and all you can live for is the future."

"I am doing my absolute best, not repeat old habits," Massai states.

"Yeah, me too," Brian replies. "By the way, Joh, how are things with you and Paris?"

"It's a long road, with a whole lot of making up to do. But I think we might just make it after all."

"I hope you do, 'cause she's well worth it," Massai says. "And I should know. I blew it with her. Not for nothing, but that is what prison life will do to you. If you let it, it will make you lose sight of what you have, thinking there's more out there to get."

"Yeah, I know," Brian responds, thinking about the mistake—that huge mistake—he made with Alanna. "Sometimes, you never get the chance to go back and make it right. I didn't! I admit I screwed up royally on this last one. If you find it, get it, hold on to it. It doesn't always come back."

They all knew exactly what Brian was talking about and why he needed to say what was on his mind. He had messed up in a big way. She was Alanna's sister, and even though she was eighteen years old,

Jennifer was her sister, living in the same house with them. He knew it's hands-off territory. *If it wasn't for the promises they made to one another to maintain the brotherhood no matter what, they would have deaded his ass a long time ago.*

"So . . . tell us," Joh says, changing the subject, "do you have a special woman in *your* life, Massai?"

"I do," he responds, hoping his face didn't give anything away. "She's an old friend of a friend, so she's not comfortable with the transition yet. But she's exactly what I need right now in my life, and I think I'm the same for her. We've both been through some changes, and those changes have made us better. I've been seeing her for the past three months, and it's been great."

"Three months! And the friend has no idea?" Ian looks shocked.

"No, she doesn't. And I'm afraid of what she'll do when she finds out."

"Well," Brian adds, "have you and this girl ever been intimate with one another?"

"Because you're my brothers, I am going to answer that question, but you're being kind of personal right now," Massai states.

"I am sorry, brother. My bad, He said, she said." Brian replies.

"No! Even though I want too. We've decided to wait a while. Don't get me wrong: a brother just came home and is ready, but like I said, I've grown, and a grown man can wait."

"Okay . . . I heard and respected that! A man should never tell his business, especially about his woman," Ian jumps in.

"No?" Joh asks, stunned.

"No!" Massai confirms. "We've been taking our time. Lately, it's been all about moral support and building our friendship."

"Sounds like you're moving in the right direction," Ian adds.

"How would you know, Mr. Perfect Married Man?" Brian shoots back.

"Do I detect some animosity—or should I say . . . jealousy?"

"Not everybody can have what you and Egypt got."

"Oh, yes, they can! You just have to work at it. And remember, not only does all that good stuff matter, but when the lights go out in the bedroom, let just say "keep that part equally important too," Ian says with a laugh.

"Yeah . . . man!" Massai states.

"You've been away in prison a long time, my brother, but not long enough to know what I'm talking about." Ian winks.

"I know. But back to the issue at hand," Massai continues. "I really want to tell Pa—I mean . . . umm . . . "

"What? What did you just say?" Ian says, jumping at Massai's slip of the tongue.

"Paris, is it?" Brian asks.

"No," Massai responds hastily, knowing he just blew his cover.

"She is not only her friend but someone she considers a sister, Massai?" Joh adds.

"Well . . . ummm . . . yes," Massai admits reluctantly.

"Paris?" Brian asks.

"Yes," Massai replies.

"I know Paris. She is not going to take this well. She hates betrayal. You should know, Massai. You've known her longer than any of us. Since you, it took her a long time to get to where she is right now," Joh states.

"I know what you mean," Brian replies.

"Well, not for nothing, little brother," Ian chimes in. "Paris is a big girl, and I'm sure she'll be okay once she gets over the initial shock of it."

"I hope so. I had never wanted to hurt her honestly. After her, it took a minute, but I finally found someone I can relate to and possibly love. In the words of Paris, life goes on whether you participate in it or not."

"Yup . . . that sounds like Paris." Joh laughs.

"But before I tell you guys who it is, Brian, I need to speak to you alone. Excuse me," Massai states.

"Yeah, sure. Order me another beer, Ian," Brian asks.

Ian consents while Massai and Brian head toward the end of the bar.

"Brian," Massai begins, "I need to tell you something, and I don't want you to hear this from anyone else. I've been seeing Alanna."

"I know," Brian responds. "I've seen you two together, only you didn't see me. I'm not mad. I can't be jealous or hurt. I was a fool, and I let her go. Life goes on. Do your thing, just don't hurt her. She doesn't deserve that. I've done enough," Brian adds.

"I promise you, my brother, I have no intention of hurting her. I just wanted you to hear it from my mouth first," Massai states.

"I appreciate that, brother. Step to it—it's all yours."

As the brothers go back to the table, the other two can't help but wonder what they were talking about. Ian states, "You good?"

"Yes, we're just catching up on some things. It's all good," Massai states.

"Are you good, Brian?" Joh asks.

"Yeah . . . we good. What y'all drinking?"

"Hennessey and ginger ale," Ian replies.

"Just give me a Hennessey straight up," Brian states.

"You sure you good?" Ian asks again.

"Yes, he is good. If you must know, I've been seeing Alanna, and I just wanted him to hear it from me first. Can we change the subject?" Massai

states.

"Hell no, we just getting started," Ian adds.

"I'm afraid I'll have to give her some time to get used to us as a couple." "Couple?" Ian says.

"Yes," Massai responds.

"And Brian, you're okay with this?"

"Yeah, I gave him the okay," Brian replies.

"Let me ask you a question, Massai," Ian says.

"What?"

"Anybody thought about how Paris will feel?" Ian asks.

"Yes. I have, but she is now with Joh. I doubt if she will really care," Massai replies.

"So, you didn't speak with Paris yet?"

"No, Paris is not my mother, and I don't have to talk with her. We grown in this life. What we had is over." Massai's voice rises.

"For someone who acts like he doesn't care, it sure doesn't look that way. Are you sure you good? Maybe you want to give Paris a call. We got you, brah." Ian chuckles.

"Oh, I see you got jokes. Let me worry about my business, brother. I appreciate your concern, but we good on every level, brah." Massai smiles back.

"Okay, are you ready to make her a part of your daily routine, your responsibilities?" Ian continues as the oldest and most respected of the brothers. He feels the need to make sure Massai knows exactly what he is getting into.

"I'm not sure what you mean, Ian."

"Women like consistency. More importantly, they like for you to talk to them, ask them about their day, etc. It's an investment."

"It may have been a while, but I am not a complete fool. And stop preaching to me. I'm good. We good! No need to worry. Can we change the subject?" Massai says angrily.

"I've been at this a lot longer than you have. I wanna know if you're ready because they are already a family. You know her sister lives with her," Ian states.

"Well, since you put it that way," Massai says with a laugh, "my *BIG* brother Ian! Ha ha ha! To answer your question, "YES", I'm ready to make her a part of my daily routine, a part of my mental thoughts, and, more importantly, a part of my responsibilities."

"I hear you, brah," Ian states.

"Ah, when you say 'responsibilities,' you just meant "call and check-in, from time to time,' right?" he adds with a smile.

"If need be," Ian says, not picking up on the sarcasm. "Yes! It also means paying some bills too. It's the small things that matter. No one wants to feel used, brah!"

"I got it, man. I was joking with you. It went over your head as usual." *Ian has no sense of humor,* Massai thinks but chuckles half-jokingly and half-appreciatively. *If I didn't know my responsibilities as a man before this, I damn sure know them now."*

"Yeah, listen, I gotta go, man, I am running late. Massai states.

"Why are you leaving?" Ian asks.

Brian thinks, *I've made a big mistake this time, but the next time love shows up, I'll be ready! 'Cause Lord knows it's lonely at the top, middle, and bottom especially when you have no one to share it with.*

"Listen, I gotta go, too Brian adds".

"Are you leaving too?" Ian asks.

"I got to get up early in the morning", Brian replies

Yes, I promised Alanna I would stop by before I head home."

"Yeah, I see. I understand." They give each other a pound as Massai walks away.

*Well . . . that went well,* Ian thinks and pays the tab. Enough said.

## SHE SAID

*She never asked me, but I told her anyway.*
*And I never wanted to, but she said I could.*
*I dared you to understand, and I dared her*
*To take me there; she said I would enjoy it as long*
*As I'm not afraid.*

*And so, I told her never to change the true essence of who she*
*was because only I would know of who she really was. She said, okay!*

*I promised to remain his forever, and he said he'd do the same.*
*So tell me: when did it all change? If we made promises we*
*said we'd keep, then how did we get here?*
*She said life has a way of us teaching a few good lessons, and one of them*
*was never make promises you can't keep—especially to*
*her because she'll always remember what was said*
*I'll live and die for my word every day. It's a street code but*
*one a woman never understands, because of what I said.*

*Life has a way of teaching us a few good lessons. As for love, it has*
*taught me how to love—But this time only smarter and wiser!*

# TOMORROW

*I remember the day I laid eyes on Mr. Massai, and he was looking deliciously rugged, tall, handsome, all at the same time. I was walking by—I saw his reflection in the mirror, and I couldn't contain myself. I had a mental orgasm standing up! Did I say how handsome he was? I was in love.*

"Girl!" Paris says aloud to Alanna. "*Oh my god!* Are you listening to me?"

"What? Yes," Alanna responds.

"Massai saw me standing there, acting like a fool. He started laughing at me. And I suddenly realized I was not alone in my thoughts of forbidden fruit. I told you some of the stories—but not all of it. What transpired when I met him was . . . basically, he came over trying to act as though I wasn't standing there. He walked right past me and then turned around to ask me if I was all right because I seemed a little out of place."

"Oh?" Alanna says.

"Yeah, he was a gentleman." Paris laughs. "And at the same time, he was checking me out *on the down low.* He'd asked me my name, and we made small talk—you know, 'where are you from, where do you work, etc.' He then asked to exchange numbers, but I hardly knew him. I got his number though. I told him I would call later."

"Did you?"

"Yes, girl, did I! In under two hours, I just couldn't wait any longer. He acted surprised, but he knew I was cheesing . . . of course, being a *man*, he had to play it off. He was waiting too but acted as though he wasn't expecting it. But girl, I could care less! He was sexy and rugged at the same time. He turned me on instantly. I was drooling all over *a* brother. Even though I just met him."

"Umm . . . I know the feeling. What ended up happening?" Alanna states.

"Well, we exchanged some more pleasantries," Paris continues, lost in her memories. "And as time went by, we fell in love . . . not wanting to leave each other's arms. But what I didn't know, he was still wrapped up in the streets. He was torn between me, the streets, and it soon gave way—I ended up losing the battle of the streets. Massai eventually went away for a long time. But I must say I missed him. When he was with me, he made me feel as though the sun rose and set on me. And he *always* treated me like a lady."

"Paris, I remember how much Massai meant to you, and I know how you feel or felt about him. There is something I want to talk to you about," Alanna states.

"Is everything okay? Something is off with you, Alanni!"

"Yes and no!"

"Have you been *talking* to Tameko lately? What's the yes and the no?"

"Ha ha. I don't know what you mean."

"What I mean, Alanna? How would you know what I'm feeling? Excuse me, I've only known you all my life." Paris says, surprised and annoyed. *How could Alanna possibly know how I felt—about a man she's never met?* "I've never introduced you to Massai," Paris replies.

"Yes, I know, but you talked about him a lot, but there's something I need to tell you," Alanna says nervously.

"What's wrong? I'm listening."

"Well, Paris, you and I have been friends and sisters for a long time. I've heard all your stories and cried all your tears with you."

"Get to the damn point, Alanna," Paris snaps, getting a sinking feeling in her stomach.

"Girl! I am!" Alanna responds.

"*Girl*, I am *what*?" Paris raises her voice.

"Why are you yelling at me?" Alanna says as she steps back, suddenly afraid that Paris might slap the shit out of her.

"Because I don't like the way this is sounding."

"Well . . . I . . . I understand how you felt about Massai . . . because I feel it now too," Alanna says timidly.

"*Too?*" Paris responds. "What do you mean . . . too?"

"Well . . . we've been seeing each other for the past three months," Alanna says cautiously. "And I've grown to like him. I might even love him."

"Love him?" Paris begins to feel an ache in her chest like she's never felt before. She never thought one of her best friends would do something like this.

"I'm sorry . . . " Alanna says.

"What. Sorry? Massai?"

"Yes," Alanna answers. "He's all that you said he was, I just never thought I would meet him in person. One day I was at the laundry, washing clothes. We noticed each other from across the room, and it took flight from there. By the time we folded our last loads of clothing, we had realized that we knew some of the same people and wanted to know more about each other."

"You can't be serious right now," Paris states.

"He told me that he once loved this woman very much, who was a lawyer and a poet, and, well, I couldn't help but soon realized we knew the same woman. You! But it was too late. We wanted to get to know each other."

"NOT LONG ENOUGH, APPRENTLY," Paris shouts back.

"We tried to ignore our feelings for each other, but as time went by, we couldn't any longer. We gave into our emotions, and the rest is history."

"So, *that's* why your ass has been acting a little crazy lately, not really wanting to talk to me, get together and shit. Alanna? I can't believe this shit! You of all people! I would expect this from Tameko, but not you!"

"I'm sorry. That is why I wanted to tell you first. I didn't want you running into us or to see us walking down the street without talking to you. We did not want you to feel like we're betraying you. I don't want to hurt you, Paris."

"Yeah, well, I'm pissed."

"Listen, my friendship means more to me than any man. I'm your girl for life, and if this bothers you or you feel disrespected, then it's over between us. He knows that."

"Really. Okay!"

"Umm, seriously." Alanna stutters.

"Yes. Damn it. I loved him. He was my first love. I don't want him with my friends." Paris's voice rises.

"I thought—"

"You thought I would just give you my blessings. Not."

"It's just, how I was to know we'd have a mutual friend who happened to be my best friend? Damn!" Alanna says.

"Damn, girl, that's a lot to take in. Just a few minutes ago I was reminiscing on about how special this man was to me, and now you're telling me . . . he's your dude," Paris states.

"I am sorry if that made you uncomfortable," Alanna responds.

"It's okay. Honestly, Massai was a long time ago, and when he came home, I was tired of waiting. It was time to move on."

"He is really a changed man and doing his best to be a better man," Alanna says.

"I know. He called, and we talked," Paris answers.

"Oh, okay," Alanna states.


"Why are you talking to me about Massai, Alanna? Is there something you want to tell me?"

"About us?" Alanna asks.

"US?" Paris asks.

"Yes?"

"Is there an owl in here? What the hell is going on. Why would he be talking to me about you? He never mentioned your name! *He would never bring that topic up to me.*" Paris's voice rises again.

"Well, ah, maybe I should be going then." Alanna turns and prepares to leave.

"Wait! You're not going anywhere . . . what is going on? You clearly have something to tell me about you and Massai."

"Yes, let me just say it. We've been seeing each other."

"WHAT? For how long?"

"It's been awhile. "

"A while? What's a while?"

Three months. Alanna replies

I guess that is why he didn't tell me. He knows I wouldn't have taken it well."

"I understand if you are upset," Alanna answers.

"Upset, girl he was my first true love

I know. That is why I was afraid to talk with you, but I didn't want you to be surprise if you saw us walking around.

Honestly, I never thought one of my friends would be dating him... out all the men in the world...Massai? "

"I am sorry, Paris. I hope I didn't hurt you. That was not my intention."

"Girl, the truth is what we had was kids' stuff. He will always be in my heart. Besides, me and Joh are back together and working hard to make it work. BUT . . . if me and Massai had a sexual relationship, then I would have told your ass *hell no*! You couldn't have shared in that with me."

"I understand." Alanna laughs. "And if it makes you feel better, we haven't done it yet. I was waiting to tell you first. Because like I said, if you are still having a problem, then it's over instantly."

"You mean to tell me you haven't dipped into the water yet?" Paris asks with some surprise in her voice.

"Nope," Alanna answers.

"Why?" Paris is surprised.

"I know it's hard to believe—he is so gorgeous—but we both wanted to tell you first, grow our friendship, and see where it goes. Besides, I got baggage."

"Yeah, you do, and thank you," Paris answers. "I love you too. *Honestly, if it had been Tameko, she would've slept with him, bragged about how big his dick is, and told me how much of a fool I was to let him go? I would have had to kick her ass off-from the jump."*

"Ha ha. Yep . . . that sounds like something she would do and then throw it in your face, *"Tameko, nasty ass"*. No, seriously, do we have your blessing?" Alanna asks.

*In my mind, it doesn't really bother me. I just wanted her ass to sweat a little.* Paris chuckles. "I guess I have to be mature about this.

Paris are you still here? Alanna notices her dazing off

I'm sorry, in my thoughts. Like I said, we were kids. Nothing really happened anyway." Paris smiles. "You have my blessing."

"Thanks, big sis," Alanna says.

"But Alanna . . . "

"Yeah?"

"Do me a favor. Don't discuss your personals with me—yet. Massai was very special to me, and I don't think I can handle that right now," Paris says, trailing off in her mind. *Because I always wanted to taste him, bathe with him. I had plans with him. I always imagine what it would have been like just, the thought of what that could've felt like, shit.* "If I could change the hands of time, leaving our tomorrows behind . . . " Paris forgets Alanna is still in the room as she speaks aloud walking in the bedroom.

*"Excuse me, biatch, but that is my man you're* sexualizing over. I can hear you," Alanna interjects.

"I'm sorry, just leave me out of the particulars for a while, that's all," Paris responds, blushing slightly.

"Okay, deal." Alanna chuckles. *I'm glad I got that off my heart and mind,* she thinks. *I can finally begin to relax. I've waited three months to be alone with this man, and before that, it was a least six months of no intimacy for me with anyone.*

"If you don't mind, I'm finished with this conversation, and like I said, I don't want to hear your intimate details either," by the way, how is your sister? Paris ask.

"No problem. I am not ready to share. Anyhoo, my sister's therapy is going well, and the yesterdays are no longer a part of my tomorrows. Today, I look forward to being more than friends."

"Okay, girl. It's all good, and I am glad we talked. I will see you soon, more sooner than later. Let's end with this poem for you. Ha ha."

"Good night, sis." Alanna walks out and closes the door. *I am so glad that conversation is over. Now, I can look forward to being with my man and looking forward to tomorrow, too.*

# TOMORROW

*It is a grain of sand in my hand*
*It is the glow of the light and at the*
*Blink of an eye, as I sit and wonder*
*What it all means to me.*
*I love to run my fingers through*
*Your hair, slide my fingers along your*
*Back and reminisce on the feelings*
*Of what all this is to me.*
*Being within my reach*
*It is the desires of love mystifying, the emotions*
*Of what love has conquered.*
*We used to sit and dream of our future together.*
*Now that it has arrived, I am*
*Still, by your side, unmistakenly dreaming*
*Of the day you become mine in the visions of*
*Tomorrows behind.*

# SUBMISSIVELY YOURS

*The moment I saw Massai,* Alanna thinks, *I just wanted to fall to my knees and polish him off something lovely, just because I like that shit. However, of course, being the woman I am, I could not very well have done that. But . . . I am so happy I finally told Paris about Massai and me. I don't think I could have kept that secret quiet much longer. Oh! There goes the phone.*

"Hello?"

"Hey, baby, it's me."

"Hi, baby, I was just thinking about you."

"You were, were you?" Massai responds. "And what was on your mind?" He's using that seductive voice, hoping his baby girl gets the message.

"You'll know once you get over here, my man," Alanna says, letting Massai know that she hears and feels him—loud and clear.

"Over here? Where?"

"Over to my place! *Hear the melody in my voice,*" Alanna says.

"I do, and I like," Massai says.

"Okay, baby! Later!"

She hangs up the phone, but a moment later, it's ringing again. *"Who could this be?"* Alanna's voice seems stressed.

"Hello, Alanna, are you there? It's me, Paris."

"Paris? What's up? I am surprised to be hearing from you. Are you okay?"

"Yes, I am fine. Who were you just on the phone with?" Paris asks.

"Excuse me, I don't have to answer that," Alanna states.

"Yes, but *with whom* you were talking. I hope it wasn't Massai."
Paris finds herself being nosy.

"I am sorry, what's with the twenty questions, and why are you in
my business? I am sorry, but we discussed this, Paris," Alanna says.

"I just asked!"

"Okay. If you must know, it was Massai. Not that I need to explain
myself to you," Alanna states.

"Oh, sorry, I asked," Paris replies.

"No, it is okay, but is everything okay with you? I am afraid you've
been distant lately. We still have your blessing?"

"Yes, you do, Alanna. Believe me, it's not you."

"Then what is it?" Alanna asks.

"I don't know. Lately, I've just been in a shitty mood," Paris says.

"Is everything all right with you and Mr. Joh?"

"Yes, it's perfect," Paris says with a secretive smile. "But I am missing
something, and I don't have a clue as to what it might be. I can't put
my finger on it. Anyhoo, have you seen or spoken to Tameko lately?"

"Not lately. Is everything all right?" Alanna says.

"Yeah." *But she's been distant too,* Paris thinks.

"Paris? Are you still there?"

"Yes . . . just thinking my thoughts out loud in my head. Well," she
continues briskly, "if you see Tameko, tell her to call me. I got to go.
Talk to you later."

"Okay, bye, talk to you later." *That was strange,* Alanna thinks.

Paris hangs up.

*Well,* Alanna thinks, *now it's time for me to get ready for my man.
Tonight is the night for some lovemaking. I've wanted to make love to this
man for a long time now. Hard and soft, sensual, and long. It's been a
long time coming. Submissively yours is all that matters to me right now.
Tonight is the night.*

\*\*\*

*Oh damn,* Massai thinks. *Somebody's at the door. I'm not ready yet, and I have to be going soon. Whoever it is, it better damn well be a good reason.*

"Hello? Who's there?"

"Paris. It's me, Massai. Open the door."

"Paris?"

"Yes, Massai. I need to talk to you. Do you mind?" Paris asks.

"No. Come in. I was just about to leave, but I have a minute. What's up, girl?"

"Are you expecting someone?"

"No, but I'm about to leave. I'm going out."

"Well, I won't take much of your time. I just wanted to talk to you for a moment. I wanted to make sure I'm making the right choice."

"Choice? What are you talking about?" Massai looks surprised. "What choice is that?"

"I don't know. I'm just . . . "

"Just what?"

"How do you feel about me, Massai?"

"What? What do you mean? We are friends, you and I."

"Just say it."

"Damn, girl. You come all this way over here in the heat of the moment when I'm about to leave, and you're asking me how do I feel about you and I."

"Yes," Paris answers, afraid and almost unaware of what she is doing.

"Well, if you must know, I still love you dearly and I always will. But the man I am today belongs to someone else, and I truly believe that I love her now, and I thank you for that."

"Do you ever wonder . . . well . . . that if we had given it another chance, it could have worked?"

"I don't know. Maybe it would've. But it's neither here nor there. But we'll always be friends," he adds. "Paris, *what is going on with you?*"

"I don't know, Massai. I guess I'm already having prewedding jitters, and I wanted to be sure I was making the right decision."

"Prewedding jitters?" Massai asks, feeling a little confused.

"As you know, Joh and I are back together. And he asked me to marry him, and I said yes."

"Oh. Congratulations. But, umm . . . what does that have to do with me?"

"After you, Massai, I wasn't sure if I could ever love another man. Honestly, I had given up on ever finding love again."

"I remember, Joh. We met a long time ago but fell out of contact with him since I been away. I knew him when we were kids. The guys and I met up with him the other night. We talked and he sounded serious about the two of you. And of course, I'm with Alanna, as you know."

"Yes, I do," Paris says a little sarcastically.

"I thought you were okay with us," Massai states.

"I am. Maybe not, but it is too late. I do love Joh, but I loved you once too."

"Paris, why are you here? I am confused." Massai asks, not understanding Paris's motives.

"Because you were my first love, Massai. I wanted to be sure I was over you—because we never really gave our love a chance, and I don't want to have any regrets."

"Look, Paris, I let you get away, I'll admit that, but today, we both moved on and have found new loves."

"I know," Paris adds.

"Well, since you moved on, then why are you here? You know we'll always be friends, and I promised never to forget what we meant to each other, but I moved on, and so have you, Paris."

"I understand," Paris responds. *"There's no sense in rehashing old ghosts. We gotta let sleeping dogs lie. Sometimes, I think about what could have been, but I know it's over,* Massai."

"Paris, you're a beautiful woman who has a lot to offer, and Joh will be pleased with his leading lady. And if you want my blessing, there you have it," Massai responds, hoping to give Paris a sense of closure.

"Maybe that's what I wanted or needed, Massai. Your blessing."

"Well, if that's all it takes, then go ahead and get married! I am letting you go, Paris. I love you always, my friend."

"How about you, Massai? Do you want to get married?"

"Yes, and I will—once I finish putting the pieces in my life together. I want to make my woman very happy too."

"You've definitely grown into the man I knew you could become, Massai. I am proud of you," Paris states.

"Yes, and I owe a lot to you, Paris, and to my special lady. It's time I grew up and became the man I know I can be. When I think about love, it's her. And when I think about being submissive, it's to her. So yes, I'm ready to become the man who's ready to anchor a woman and make her feel safe. I am ready."

"Life has taught you a few good lessons, I see. And I must say I'm impressed," Paris replies.

"Some of the credit belongs to you, Paris, but this time, being behind the concrete wall . . . you have no choice but to listen to your inner thoughts. It will force you to slow down and take note. I had to tear down the old me so I can rebuild and become this new person I can respect."

"You give me too much credit, Massai, and I don't deserve it."

"There you go, being modest again," he says with a laugh. "You know, you share *some* responsibility for the man I've become. I wouldn't be here if you hadn't closed the door in my face and forced me to get myself together."

"I didn't close the door in your face, man. Or did I?"

"Yes, you did. And you were rather rude too, ha ha. But I am not mad at you." Massai laughs again.

"Well, enough conversation. I've got a wedding to plan, I'm glad we talked," Paris states.

"I am too. We are both happy now. Thank you for stopping by," Massai replies.

*Paris kisses Massai on the cheeks and closes the door behind her. In her mind, she thinks it's hard to be submissive to someone, and they become yours to love again. The completion is the commitment, and the poem goes like this.*

# SUBMISSIVELY YOURS

*When I decided to merge my soul*
*With yours, I never thought that the depths of*
*My inner being would resemble the smile upon your*
*Face.*
*There's a quiet place within me and it's*
*Laced with quiet storms, melodic moves,*
*And a bouquet of juices flowing just for you!*
*You said one more time, and I said okay.*
*Relinquish yourself to me; I am ready to go there*
*To the place, where the sun runneth down my back*
*Along with the moistness of your lips. Glisten my body*
*With your luscious tongue, blanket me with your*
*unconditional love*
*And I promise that whatever happens I am yours totally and*
*Completely, never to return, because in the end, it's just you and I*
*Passionately, personifying, intimately expressing, and the joy of what we*
*have together! I am submissively yours.*

# MAN TALK

Joh walks into the barbershop where most men go to hang out, bond, and talk smack. It's a sacred place—"Switzerland," a place where men get to talk about their issues, and it doesn't leave the shop. They discuss things only concerning them. Just as Massai is about to leave, Joh notices him as he is about get out of his seat and yells, "Hey, brother, hold up for a minute."

Massai, startled, thinks, *Why would this dude want to talk to me? I never met him before. Excuse me?*

"Hold up. Can I talk with ummmm for a minute?" Joh asks again.

"Excuse me, I don't think we've met. Do I know you, my brother?" Masai replies.

"No, but I know you, and of course, we know some of the same people. Let me introduce myself. My name is Joh."

"Yeah, and who would that be? Seeing we never met before," Masai answers.

"You know Paris and her girl, Alanna. They are friends, and we all hang out sometimes," Joh answers.

"You know Paris. Oh, I see."

"Yes. We've been talking for a minute now."

"Oh yeah. And you hang out with Alanna, how? She is . . . " Massai says.

"I know who Alanna is to you. As I said, I know Paris. She talked about you. You used to be close friends. I know all about you and your relationship."

"Oh, really?"

"Yes."

"And what is it do you know? And what does this have to do with Alanna? Nothing, really. Just Paris and I ….

Paris and you, what? I am not sure why you are stepping to me, brother," Masai states.

"I just wanted to talk with you. I'm not trying to get into your business. We know some of the same people, and when we are all around each other, I don't want it to be awkward," Joh answers.

"Awkward? I don't follow."

"Paris and I seeing each other. I thought you should know."

"I don't need to know Paris's business, and who she sees or not, is not any of my concern! We are old friends, and that is it! Brother, we don't talk about our women this way. I'm from the streets, and this type of conversation doesn't happen between two men or men in general."

"I understand that. I am not trying to get into your business, as I stated. I just want to introduce myself, if and when we should cross paths."

"Really. Okay, my brother. Like I said, Paris and I are good. And as for Alanna, that is my business. I don't discuss my woman with no man. That is not how we do things. You understand?"

"Yes. I get that. Of course, that goes for Paris and me. She doesn't know we are speaking and so I want to keep this between you and I. "

"Paris? I know she didn't send her man to talk to me. That is not like her.

"No, she didn't send me. I am a man. I just wanted to talk with you myself. Later, brother," Joh says.

We don't have to continue with this conversation. Tell her we good. It's all good, and when we see each other again, no worries," Massai states.

"I understand, brother. I appreciate the Man- talk, we need to have more of this but not like this. I can't get with this. " Masai mumbles as he walks out the door.

"Yeah, see you later brother. I am with that." Joh awkwardly responds.

# MAN TALK

It's the small talk we have inside the barbershops, standing
on the corner, and in those rare moments, punch each
other in the face, yet we understand each other.
Man Talk is about my brother, my friend, and my enemy. It is
the small exchange of words that only we can understand.
Our conversation can be aggressive, strong, and
abrasive, but nonetheless, we embrace every part
of what that brings. It's our way of talking.
We don't waste time with idle conversations and even when
we don't talk for long periods of time, we still embrace each
other as if time never lapsed. Our friendships are long-lasting.
We will hold each other down, stand for one another, Die for
one another, Our word is everything. Behold this bond!
Sometimes it does not require any exchange of words,
it's a pound on the back, fist bumps or even a small
hug, tells men everything they need to know.
When they speak, only in their native tongue; the unspoken
love is translated between men, and this establishes
their Man Talk; it's only for them to understand.

# RIGHT HERE, RIGHT NOW

"Dang, baby! What took you so long?" Alanna asks.

"Paris stopped by. I was surprised to see her. She wanted to talk," Massai responds.

"Oh, she did. And what about?" Alanna's voice seems concerned.

"Yes, she wanted to make sure old ghosts were gone. And I think she wanted my blessing for her and Joh to get married."

"Oh, I see," Alanna says, relieved. She was nervous that Paris still had a hold on her man.

"What's going on in that pretty head of yours, baby girl?" Massai asks.

"Nothing, baby. I . . . "

"Oh, I know you're wondering if I'm still carrying a torch for Paris."

"She was very important to you, Massai."

"She was, but that is over and we're good now. She has moved on, and so have I."

"I know, but I don't want any issues moving forward with us," Alanna states.

"Well, if you need to know, just put your hand on *my* torch, and I'll show you just who it desires. I've waited a long time for you, woman, and old ghosts have no place in my world anymore."

"Keep talking, Daddy. I like the sound of that," Alanna replies. "You right—we've all moved on, and there's no sense in worrying about what was when we can concentrate on what can be. Right here, right now is the only place I want to be, Daddy."

"Daddy. I like the sound of that. Say it again!" Massai responds, begging a little. "You're making me so hard, I'm afraid I might hurt you," he whispers in her ear.

"Hurt me?" Alanna whispers back, laughing. "I've been waiting for this since the day I laid eyes on you in that laundromat! But out of respect, we had to take care of some unfinished business first. Let me arch my back and then . . . do what you do . . . Daddy."

"Let's stop all this talking and start TCB-ing."

"TCB-ing?" Alanna asks.

"Taking care of business, ha ha." Massai smiles at Alanna's innocence.

As they melt into each other's arms, it all becomes crystal clear. They had found each other after so much turmoil in their lives, and they knew they were ready to take care of each other in every way imaginable.

Massai also knew that it was almost time to ask the question. Because the woman lying next to him was all he needed. There was no sense in prolonging it but tying up loose ends was taking longer than he expected. He also knew he wanted his home to be happy, then all matters needed to be resolved. Right here, right now was all that really mattered. And . . . the smell of this woman lying next to him made it worth the struggle to maintain and play his position in a poetic way "I remember this poem in my head. It went something like this!"

# RIGHT HERE, RIGHT NOW!

*Right here, right now, is all that really matters to me?*
*Never could I have arrived at this very moment without you in my presence.*
*I must be the luckiest person in the world to have loved so divinely.*
*I romanced your touch upon my body, and I play with the thoughts of what that*
*Feels like, and yes, I'm impressed once again.*
*Our lovemaking, the breath on my face, your fingertips crawling down my back, the moistness between my leg overwhelms my thoughts, and that's exactly why I stay.*
*Right here, right now is so damn urgent to make you smile.*
*It reminds me of what's so important and at this very moment. It's you, my love! Intensifying the sweetness and simplifying the lovemaking, never overbearing. Just sweet gestures toward me and how I make you feel.*
*Yes, I can give it to you and never expect anything in return.*
*I'm here for the taking, just for the pleasing, hard, and deep, caught up in you. Right here, right now is all that really matters to Me!*

# IMAGINATION

"I'm so happy I took your advice and respected my relationship." Egypt gets excited. "I love my husband, and I wouldn't trade him or us for nothing in the world. I don't want anything to ruin what I have or hurt my family. Let me take it back to the day I met him. He was walking down the street in a hurry. And in my low voice, I said, 'Dang, he's cute.'"

He turned around and said, "And so are you."

"I thought he didn't hear me. He was walking so fast, but he did. But he took the time to ask for my number."

"Really?" Paris says, raising an eyebrow. "*That* was simple enough." Paris is pleased her advice was taken but annoyed at how Egypt's always trying to rewrite history.

"Whatever. I'm sensing some shade on your part," Egypt responds.

"No, no, no! I remembered all too well how you met Ian. Remember? We were walking together. And I do believe you are right about saying he was cute. But if memory serves me correctly, *you* were the one who offered your number to *him*. You actually ran up to him and suggested he take your number, missy."

"I did not!"

"Yeah, you did. You damn near crammed it down his pockets. You were so beside yourself that day. I was surprised."

"Really?! No, I didn't!" Egypt responds, embarrassed. "Well, I guess I did . . . I couldn't help it. I don't know I just had this feeling about him. As it turns out, I wasn't wrong. We've been together ever since that day."

"You were so nervous, and you weren't even sure if he called. It took him about two weeks before you heard from him. And by that time, you were moping around like some lost puppy."

"I can admit, I was a mess!" Egypt says, being more truthful now. "I just knew he was the one. And again, I was right."

"I must say, you were right. Ian is a charming guy, father, and husband. Do you remember calling me every day because he hadn't called and trying to act like you didn't care."

"I was a mess for someone I hardly knew, but it felt right. When it's right, you know. I wanted to get to *know* him. Not to mention all these feelings all at one time it was crazy . . . it felt like I'd fallen in love at first sight. Paris, I know you understand. I mean, right?"

"I understand," Paris responds. "I had a love like that once. Unfortunately, it didn't last. I wanted it, but it just didn't work out. He went away, and love went with him until I met Joh . . . "

"That's good . . . yeah . . . But anyway, getting back to my story about Ian."

*Classic Paris . . . somehow, she always finds herself in the storyline,* Egypt thinks.

*I wish she'd hurry up with this damn story. It's not like we don't know the ending: she marries him! Happy ever after,* Paris thinks.

"As I was saying, I thought he wasn't going to call me," Egypt continues. "It was about two weeks at this point, and my imagination had gotten the best of me."

"Seriously? Are we still talking about fifteen years ago? You married the man. What else is there to talk about?" Paris replies, half-teasing and half-annoyed.

"As I was saying, I was becoming frustrated because I hadn't heard from him. I thought I had played myself—but then the phone rang. Ian's on the other end."

"What are we revisiting in the past, Egypt? I don't get it." Paris says, annoyed.

"Honestly, I love telling our love story. Ah, where was I? Oh, yes, we talked about history, current events, etc. He was a breath of fresh air, mainly because I kept meeting the same type of dudes. I remember like it was yesterday. He liked the fact that I was direct and to the point, and I like the *fact that he listened. Not all men can appreciate the forwardness and directness of a woman, Paris."*

"*I know what you mean. Joh and I have always had an open and honest relationship until our incident. Since then, I have become a better communicator, and he still listens to me. Ha ha,"* Paris states.

"*When Ian and I started talking, our conversation was heavy from the beginning. I remember him going straight from the beginning. He asks me, 'Who are you?'"*

"And you said . . . "

"'*I am Egypt, a graduate of Fordham University, business major, single woman, and about her business!'*

'*What will you do with that business degree, once your graduate? If I may ask?'*

'*I thought about artist management. I like the music business and want to build up the artist. I love the business or maybe law school.'*

'*I see!'*

'*You see what?'*

'*That you're ambitious. That's a rare quality to find in most young women.'*

'*You sound like you're an old man.'*

'*On the one hand, I'm twenty-three years old. But my life started a little earlier than most young men my age.'*

'*What do you mean?'*

'*Before I answer your question, I haven't gotten all my questions answered yet.'*

'*Okay, Ian. Bring it on!'* I like his leadership. I like being handled, Egypt thinks.

'*Such directness. I really like that in a woman.'* He laughs.

'*There you go again, sounding like an old man,'* I reply. '*You're just barely twenty-three years old, and you sound like you've lived a whole life. I can only imagine what your childhood was like.'*

'*No, not yet. We're still on you—where are you going? I understand you want to work in the music business, but is that all you really want for yourself? It doesn't sound promising.'*

'What are you trying to say?' I say, confused by his questions.

'Okay, I'll rephrase it: Where do you see yourself going? I should have been more direct too.'

'Hmmm . . . let me get back to you on that, okay? I really gotta take some time and think about it.'

'Okay. No pressure, Egypt. Just so you know, there's no wrong or right answers to any of these questions—just my way of understanding a woman that I want to get to know.'

'And here I am thinking I am the only woman you've asked these questions to.'

'No, but maybe you're the only one who'll answer them the way I want to hear them.'

'Oh,' I say, surprised by his direct manner. 'Okay. Are there any more questions?'

'No, that's it for now.'

'Okay. I gotta go, Ian.'

'Oh wait, one more: Are you seeing anyone, Egypt?'

'Yeah, I'm dating . . . but nothing serious. Why are you asking?'

'Nothing serious? What does that mean?'

'It means what I said. Just dating. Nothing serious. Just seeing what's out there, that's all."

'I see,' he says, seemingly unsure of my answers.

'If you've finished grilling me, let me ask you some questions. What's your M.O.?'

'What do you mean, M.O.? I don't understand what you're asking me.'

'It means your "make-up." What makes you the man you are?'

'Don't forget, you still have one question to answer.'

'How could I forget, Mr. Man? You won't let me. But don't think I am not listening. What is your M.O.?'

'Believe you me! I have no M.O. except to get to know who you are and what makes you smile.'

'Ummm, you seem like your dodging the question, but okay, Paris. I am talking like Ian is standing right next to me."

"Are we almost done with this story? Egypt, I got to go," Paris states.

"Ah, yes but where are you going? There's no one at your house but your cats. You are becoming a cat lady, Paris."

"No, I am not, and I don't have a cat. I'm not a cat person. Remember, my neighbor needed me to watch the cat while she went away for the weekend. Hurry up, please. Stop getting off the topic. I want to story to be over already, Egypt, damn."

"Anyhoo. He told me his name was Ian, and that he was also a graduate of Fordham."

"So, I don't care. *Okay. And?" Paris answers.*

*"Yes, he was, and then he told me that he had seen in the hallways for almost six months before graduation. He knew who I was but waiting for an opportunity to introduce himself to me," Egypt states.*

*"Six months? Great. Is this story almost over?"* Paris asks.

*"Yes. By that time, we ran into each other, he said, 'I already knew I was going to talk to you. I just had to create an opportunity to speak to you. Don't get me wrong—I'm not shy, but sometimes I get a little nervous.'"*

*"'How did you know I would talk to you, or that I wasn't seeing someone seriously—Mr. Mysterious?' I ask. 'I decided to take the chance.'"*

"I am about to say goodbye. I don't understand why you are telling me all this now. You already married Ian," Paris states.

"And then he goes into his story. I was like, what?"

*Ian states, "Ummm, well anyway, back to my M.O. I have brothers and sisters, and I'm the oldest of four. I think I want to be a lawyer, but the computer industry interests me as well. And if I marry you, then we don't need two lawyers in the family."*

*"M . . . ma—marry me? How can you make that assumption? You don't even know my last name!"*

*"Just talking to you right now is all the answers I need," Ian says. "Excuse me, but I am a hopeless romantic. I like the way you state your business. And I'm very sure of myself. But anyway, as I was saying, I like the computer field. It piques my interest. I'm considering a computer career."*

*"Well, I'm considering attending Fordham Law. And I do plan to get married to a handsome individual who shares my same tranquility of thought."*

"*I do. You know one day I asked a man and a woman, 'What could love offer to you?' The man said, 'A whole a lot.' It gives him peace, and the woman said it gives her security. If she's willing to understand her man, stand by her man, and respect her man, and never make him feel less than a man. It makes a recipe for good relationships.*"

"*As for women, it's almost the same thing. If he's willing to anchor, love her unconditionally, stand by her, they can make it together.*"

"*I know exactly what you mean, Egypt. And as for me, I look forward to giving it to you. I have confidence in knowing that I can give you a life of slow and melodic, gentle but hard, sensual, and seductive love—with a bed of roses. But don't go letting my imagination get the best of me.*"

"*You do have one.*"

"And this is where we ended our conversation. Could you imagine meeting your forever love for the very first time?" Egypt asks.

"Yes, I can, Thank GOD this story is over. Next time . . . imagine that."

# IMAGINATION

*Can you feel the stroke of my touch, my breath upon your back?*
*I can understand your need to love me, but you can't have me.*
*I'm not yours to have, your imagination dares to love me,*
*share with me, and yet our roads never cross paths.*

*Like a thief in the night, my thoughts haunt me, and my imagination*
*has gotten the best of me. Imagination! Loving immensely,*
*so dramatically, overwhelmingly . . . engulfed in the*
*tenderness of our love, lustful, and romantically moving*
*along to a rhythm of only our minds could imagine.*

*But as I move along, I can see you in my thoughts, what do you want*
*to tell me? You can't. Because why? Love. It's surprisingly beautiful,*
*unpredictable, disappointing, and yet I love*
*the touch of your lips upon mine.*
*I love you, and I just want to be with you. Imagine that if you can!*

# I AM OUT HERE ON MY OWN

"Alanna," Brian says cautiously over the phone. "I know you're surprised to be hearing from me."

"Yes, I am. And what do you want, Brian? I told you not to call me, come to my home, and stay away from Jennifer. I am about to hang up."

"No, please don't. Alanna, I need to talk to you. Give me a minute."

"What do you want? Why are you calling me?" *I should have changed my number*, Alanna thinks.

"Nothing! Why do you always think I want something? Can't I just call and check on you?"

"No, you can't!"

"Well . . . I heard you're getting married, and I wanted to be the first to congratulate you."

"Okay, you said it. I . . . "

"Please don't hang up, Alanna. I need to tell you how sorry I am for how I treated you in our relationship. I also wanted to say, I am sorry for what happened with your sister, Jennifer," Brian states.

"REALLY!" Alanna says, struggling to control her emotions. "It's been nearly THREE YEARS! And you're just NOW deciding to come back around and apologize? For nearly destroying the only family I have and trying to bring me down with you? I don't know if you knew that Jennifer was pregnant. Did you even care about my sister? You used her, left, and got her pregnant!"

"No! I did not. Yes, I cared, but I loved you! It was just sex. She was there, always there. Jennifer was always coming onto me. I didn't want to. I know I should have tried harder to resist. I am sorry for that, but I wanted a family too," Brian replies.

"She was *devastated* for having to get rid of the baby, but she knew she couldn't care for a child on her own!"

"She did what? I . . . I . . . I would have helped her!"

"Yeah, just like you helped yourself to her innocence, Brian. You *knew* how Jennifer was. She was just a child herself. She had no idea what she was doing. As I said before, you're selfish, and you cared for only yourself. Jennifer has a mind of a ten-year-old. You knew she had problems because I told you."

"I am so . . . I . . ."

"So now you show up after all this time, apologizing. Well, it's too late for sorry and your apologies. You never wanted to help me with nothing, Brian, but you knew how to help yourself to my sister's body, her innocence, and now her mental state of mind. You took advantage of her, and now you say you would have helped raise a child?"

"Yes! I've wanted a child for quite some time now. It would've forced me to get myself together, given me a reason to change. Remember, Alanna, you didn't want any children, remember?!"

"Oh, you would have changed for a baby, but you couldn't change for us. I probably would have changed my mind, but I couldn't trust anything you did or said. Honestly, that is why I didn't want children with you. I couldn't rely on you, Brian."

"I am so sorry. I am, Alanna. I loved you. It meant nothing between your sister and me. I was just stupid."

"A *child* shouldn't force you to get yourself together! And as for a family, we *had* one! You just weren't ready! Please leave with your excuses for not doing the right thing. You did what you wanted and with whom. Jennifer was innocent in all this. But it is all good now. I got a new man, and he loves me."

"You did. Good!"

"Oh, Brian! God gave me the heads up earlier, and I knew not to get pregnant with a man who cared nothing for my family or me. Did you think I didn't want children? I did—just not with you! And my intuition was *right*! The man I'm going to marry too is the one with whom I'm willing to have his child. He's responsible, and as for my sister, he understands she has a problem, doesn't judge but instead offers solutions and support. Something I could never get from you."

"Yeah! I might've heard of that guy you were going to marry. What's his name again?" Brian jokes. "Masay?"

"No! It's Massai!" Alanna responds.

"Really!" Brian responds.

"Boy, please . . . don't act like you don't know Massai. He told me you'd been boys for a while and how you left the friendship while he was away. Honestly, this relationship has nothing to do with you."

"Didn't he just come home from jail, prison? I hope he didn't drop the soap. LOL. *And now you want to go off and get married and have his baby*. Girl, you really downsized!"

"Downsized?"

"Talk about desperate! You're a beautiful woman! Why waste your time with a loser?"

"First of all, he's not a loser. Wait. Wasn't that supposed to be your boy? He told me, you and him talked. He came to you like a man, and this is how you do him? You will never be *half* the man he is. Yes, he has some shortcomings, but he is good now."

"Just be careful, you might come home, and he robs your ass. A thief is always a thief."

"And who are you to talk, Mr. False Representative? What the *hell* are you doing? I bet you're still hustling, trying to get over on people, aren't you?"

"No, I'm just trying to *survive* in this game call life! I'm out here on my own, with no family, and now I realized that I need to try and build one of my own," Brian reflects.

"YOU'RE RIGHT! WITH ALL YOUR EDUCATION, YOU'RE STILL SO DUMB. YOU'D RATHER BE OUT THERE ON THEM STREETS, HUSTLING. OUT OF ALL OUR FRIENDS, YOU'RE THE ONE WITH THE BACHELOR'S DEGREE, AND YET YOU'RE STILL LOOKING FOR A HANDOUT. Working hard was never your forte, Brian. Just begging." She couldn't help but laugh. *He thinks he's better, but the truth is . . . sooner or later, he better wake up or he'll be the one hoping to not drop the soap. LOL. Thank God it's over!*

I think call here to argue. I wanted to apologize and wish you the best. "Sometimes, investing in yourself takes real effort but you rather put it into something else. Look in the mirror, do you like what you see? Alanna ask

Nobody never did anything for me. Brian replies

"There you go with more excuses. Sooner or later, you are going to have to do the work. It's up to *you* to create your own destiny! No one is going to come and give you anything. I'm not your momma, and I can't raise a man after he is already grown as K' Michelle states. Are you finish? Alanna states

"I know you're right. I really messed up with you and your sister. Meaning, we were a family and I should have respected that. That was an all-time low, even for me. I was greedy and stupid. I lost you, and you were the best thing that ever happened to me. Is . . . is your sister, okay?"

"Yes. I got her some counseling, and I think in time, she'll be okay."

"I loved you, Alanna, and I hope you know that."

"I thought you did too—but then I realized that wasn't love. It doesn't feel the way you made me feel all these years. Listen, I gotta go, please don't call here again.

Thank you for listening to me, Alanna. I needed to tell you, I am really sorry.

I know you are, but I have since moved on.

I know you have. Alanna, I...

"Goodbye, Brian, let's just say good-bye now. I don't want to be rude and hang-up on you. " Take care.

*For the record,* Brian thinks as he hangs up the phone, *you were the best thing that ever happened to me. I was proud to be apart of a family. I learned a lot from you, even though they say (a man can't trust a woman) I was the one who could not be trusted. I violated and now I am out here on my own, denying accountability for what I've done, only to end up in the same place. Alone!*

# I AM OUT HERE ON MY OWN

I am out here on my own and the
The transition of life's expectancy has
Dulled my vision and the unspoken
Words have made me perplexed,
The jubilation of life and the roles
We must play.
I am out here on my own to understand
The definitions of words never known and
Never seen. I want to be heard by
people, I want to be respected by my peers.
I want to be respected by my woman,
I want to be understood by all. Being on my own
Has made me fortunate to the calling of words told,
And to the statements made. Who am I and what's
my purpose? I don't want to leave this world and to have
Never known.
I will work harder and longer to prove to you my
Existence, and the need to be known. Because
I am out here on my own, and I don't want anyone to have
Never known who I truly am.

# LIFE AS WE ARE

*I'm sitting here,* Tameko thinks, *wondering about all the men who have come and gone in my short little life. I am beginning to feel lonely once again as I turn the key into my place, and there's no one standing on the other side of the door. I am starting to sound like Paris, the stuff she's been trying to tell me from the beginning. At some point, we're going to have to slow down and see our lives for the way it is. I may not like the mirror images staring back at me. Shit, here I am laughing at my own humor.*

*Dang, am I really talking to myself? I've never done that before, let alone answer myself. Am I losing my mind? It's true, sometimes the loneliness gets louder than words. Thinking about the many conversations I've had with the girls, about what type of relationship I really want. It's time I tell the girls how I am feeling. I've finally found the love I really want. And I hope it goes well. Here it is goes. Let me give them a call, or maybe it can wait. I'm not quite ready as I thought.*

"Hey, baby girl . . . when I walked in, I thought I heard you talking to someone," Samantha says.

"I was. Me! I sometimes talk to myself. Ha ha. It helps me release my own thoughts out loud," Tameko answers shyly.

"Should I be concerned? You're not having one of those mental health days are you? Ah, ah, ah?"

"Oh, I see you got jokes. Ha ha. You don't have to be concerned at all. We all do it *sometimes,* talk to ourselves."

"I don't!" Samantha states as she walks into the kitchen to put on a pot of tea.

"I'LL TELL YOU WHAT . . . THE MOMENT YOU START I'LL LET YOU KNOW," Tameko yells back. "It's as natural as putting on your shoes. Let's not make a big deal of it."

"Okay, babe. Listen, I was thinking its time I met with the girls. We need to tell them about us. You talk about them all the time. I DON'T WANT IT TO BE AWKWARD IF WE RUN INTO EACH OTHER ON THE STREETS," Samantha yells.

"What! Really . . . we've never talked about when and how we were going to tell them. I just assumed it would be later than sooner. Are you sure you're ready?"

Samantha is still in the kitchen making a cup of tea. *"Hey, do you want a cup of tea?"*

"NO . . . I'M GOOD," Tameko yells back.

"You sure?" Samantha asks.

"Yes, I am sure! Umm . . . it's about time. I was waiting for you to be ready. Unless you're having a change of heart?"

"Absolutely . . . not! I am ready if you are. DO YOU WANT ME TO GO WITH YOU?" Sam yells while standing in the kitchen.

"No! I have to do this alone . . . but thank you." *She walks up to Samantha and kisses her on the ear.*

Sam turns around startled but accepted the kiss. "Heyyyy, I like that! Do that again."

Tameko kisses her again, closer to her ear where the earlobe hangs. "Is that what you want?"

"Yes, and you better stop before we are late going to the movies, Tam."

"Honestly, the movie can wait. I feel like I want some cake pie."

"No time, I've been waiting to see *Wonder Woman*, the new version, for a while. Besides this is the last week, and then it leaves the movie theater."

"Okay. Let me get ready, but I want some of *that* when I return home, babe," Tameko states.

"No worries, it's all yours. Now getting back to the conversation at hand. I am more than ready. After that whole fiasco with Joh, I never thought I would fall in love again or be with anyone. You came along at the right time, and it felt right. Tam, I am ready. How do I look, babe?

You look girl, I'm glad for some (me) time, I got a lot of reading to do before we go to the movies, tonight. " Samantha says.

"Listen, me and the girls are meeting up back here around seven before we go to the movies if that is okay with you," Tameko states.

"I don't mind, but don't think you're getting out of taking me to the movies. No matter the outcome, were going, right?" Samantha asks.

"Yes, babe. No matter what!" Tameko replies.

"Okay, then."

"Would you mind leaving for a while? Maybe walk to the store or something. I will give you call when I am closer to home. I need to talk with them alone! I'm sorry, I know it's a last-minute request, please."

"Seriously, I thought we were doing this together?"

"I know you did, but you don't know them the way I do, and I think it's best I prepare them first."

"They're not little-ass kids. They're grown-ass women. Why you pacifying them? Pull that shit out of their mouth and let them handle it," Samantha states.

"I got to handle this my way. Just be patient. We are going to the movies. You have to trust me. We can catch the late night one anyway," Tameko answers.

"Because I love you, I am going to the gym to work out. Be your ass ready when I get back. Anyhoo, I need to relieve myself of some tension away."

"Are you feeling okay?" Tameko asks.

"I am fine . . . just some work stuff," Sam replies.

Tameko then walks up behind Sam and kisses her again, this time on the back of her neck. "You taste good, babe."

"Nope. Stop! Don't try to win me over. If we are late to the movie, I am going to be pissed. Tameko, stop, you know that's my spot. Don't start nothing . . . I just might not leave."

"Good! I can't have my girl all backed up, stressed. I'm not doing my job."

"Now see, you are playing dirty. Ha ha."

"I'll call you when it's safe to come home, and then we can work out all that tension together. We are living life as we are. I am living my best life," Tameko states.

"Oh, just you or am I in that equation? I thought we were living our best life together," Sam asks.

"Absolutely, as we are together, babe. Just you and me, Life as we are" Tameko replies.

"Okay then! Talk to you later." Samantha walks out the door.

# LIFE AS WE ARE

*You may change if you*
*Accept my changes too.*
*You may have an opinion*
*If you'll accept my answers!*
*But what you may not do*
*Is change my way of living?*
*And stay as you are!*
*Ask me how I feel and what I think*
*And I'll be glad to allow you into my life*
*Trust me as I trust you and take from me what*
*You desire, touch me in a way*
*That will give me unity. Relinquish*
*My inner soul and tell me that everything is all right!*
*This is all my heart truly wants. I'll never*
*Lie to you. Fill your head with unwanted*
*Words but what I will do is give you peace of mind.*
*Eloquently Put, Justifiably Done! For you!*

# IN TOO DEEP, CAN'T
# TURN BACK, NOW!

In this moment, Tameko realizes she needs to talk with Paris and the girls. It's starting to get serious between her and Sam. Besides, she doesn't want the girls walking in on them since they all have keys to her place. Especially Paris. She hates not knowing first.

"It's me, Tameko. Paris, are you close by? I really need to talk to you and the girls. Is there something wrong with your phone? I called three times."

"It was in my side pocket, but you know I am on my way. What's going on with you, girl? I'm just two blocks away," Paris says worriedly.

"Nothing really . . . just wanted to discuss a few things with all of you before later. I'd like for once if you would all arrive on time."

"Later? It sounds serious. Should I stop and buy some wine?"

"No! I have wine, but really, I don't have time for wine and cheese tonight. What I have to say won't take long. Besides, I have to leave shortly after. So I don't want to repeat myself, twice."

"Say what twice?" Paris asks out of concern.

"It's easier if we talked all together," Tameko replies.

"Okay then! We're on our way. Should be there by six o'clock. It's only 5:30 p.m. Be easy, were almost there. Damn!"

"You know what, I changed my mind."

"No, biatch, I am on my way. Didn't I just tell you I am only two blocks away? I'm not going to turn around and go home. And I assume so is everyone else. Well, I guess we'll have that wine and cheese after all. I made some lasagna. Put it in the oven on 355 degrees. I'm leaving my office right now."

"Wait. You're not even home? Are you serious? What the hell is going on with you?" Paris's voice rises.

"No, but I work close to home. I am just five minutes away. Let yourself in. You have the key," Tameko answers.

"You cooked?" Now, Paris *knows* that something is wrong.

"Yes, I did! I don't like to cook, but I can cook. You know that," Tameko states.

"You only cook when something heavy is on your mind, Tameko."

"I know, yeah well, I've been going through it. That's how I gained all that weight in the past."

"What weight?" Paris says supportively.

"Girl! I know when I've gained weight." Tameko laughs. "Goodbye, I'll talk to you when I see you later!"

"Bye!" *I'm really nervous about talking to these ladies. They may be my friends, but they're brutal as hell.*

***

There are knocks on the door. Tameko's mouth suddenly feels dry. *I think I need a sip of this wine before I open the door. Why am I so nervous? They are just my girls. Well . . . here it goes.* "Hey ladies! How are you doing?"

"Stop with the small talk, Tameko," Egypt says impatiently as she walks in and hangs up her coat and grabs a glass of wine at the same time. "What's with the urgency? Why did we all have to rush over here?"

"Well, hello to you too, Ms. Egypt."

"Hello my ass, Tam."

"What's up?" Alanna chimes in. She also walks over to hang her coat following Egypt and sees the wine. "I guess I'll have a glass too."

"Don't start, Alanna, with your dramatics," Tameko responds.

"Where's Paris?" Egypt and Alanna state in unison.

"I thought she said she was already here." They both laughed.

"Punch Buggy." Alanna chuckles.

"See, how old are you, still playing Punch Buggy . . . really, Alanni," Egypt states.

"Whatever. If you had the chance to get me, you would have."

"Yep . . . I would. Ha ha, so watch out." Egypt and Tameko chuckle aloud.

"Why don't you all sit down and eat some cheese, crackers, fruit? And have some more wine? I cooked some lasagna."

"YOU DID WHAT?" Alanna says, surprised.

"What? You only cook when you get stressed, Tam." They notice Paris walking out of the kitchen.

"I said the same damn thing. Hey, ladies, what's up?" Paris walks over and kisses Alanna and Egypt on the cheek.

Shit you scared me to death, girl. Alanna startles responds

"Start talking, Tameko. Apparently, this ain't no damn social call," Egypt says.

"What's wrong girl? You can tell us anything. Are you okay?" Alanna asks again.

"Yes, I am fine. If I startled you all, I am sorry. It's not that serious. It's just.. . "

"Dang, Egypt! I haven't seen you in a while. Why are you so nervous?"

"I'm sorry, do I look nervous?"

"Yes!" Egypt and Alanna say in unison again. As Alanna tries to punch Buggy with Egypt but she didn't engage. Alanna smirks. "You're starting to make me a little nervous, chicka. Why are you prolonging the conversation?"

"Yes. This is not like you, Tam," Paris chimes in.

Finally, Egypt answers. "Sorry, Alanni. I just had a long day and can't wait to get home, drink a glass of wine and get in between the legs of my husband and relax."

"That's a little too much information, don't you think, Egypt?" Paris says with a laugh. "I'm glad and all . . . but *damn!*"

"I'm sorry, I guess I got a little carried away. It's this middle-age thing. It got me so horny I can't focus even at work. I think people are starting to notice my irritability. Not to mention I'm wearing my husband out!"

Tameko begins to laugh so hard and states, "Maybe it's the wine. You know me ass can't drink."

We know, they all start laughing. Alanna stay your ass over there with that "punch buggy shit". Egypt yells.

"I hear that, but I'm sure he'll be okay!" Paris states *sarcastically*.

"Can we get down to business, ladies?" Tameko yells in the air. She feels herself getting antsy. She just wants to get the conversation going. "Look, I'm afraid I can't hold my tongue any longer."

"Ok, Shit, we waiting …Tameko? Girl, you seem stressed," Paris asks.

"Here it goes . . . I LIKE WOMEN!"

"YOU *WHAT*? IN WHAT WAY? WE LIKE WOMEN," Alanna yells.

"You heard me."

"I know what I think I heard," Egypt responds, "but I'm not sure if it was what I *think* I heard. Can you say it again?"

"Yes, I like women. I'm in love with a woman." Tameko's voice shifts.

"WHAT DO YOU MEAN YOU IN LOVE? Really?" Paris asks.

"You ladies know what I mean. "I'm in too deep, can't turn back now". I like this woman in every way. Shit, do you want me to draw you a map. It's simple. I am in love," Tameko states.

"WHAT? WAIT!" Alanna can't hide her dissatisfaction.

"What? Seriously. It sounds like you've been thinking about this for a while," Egypt states.

"Really! I am surprised," Paris responds.

"Me too!" Alanna says, whipping her head around, facing Tameko and Paris. "How you go from being with men to being with women? Why, I don't understand. Are you serious?"

"Yes, for once in my life, I' m very sure about this. Honestly, this is not my first encounter with a woman. When I was in college, during my freshman year, I met this woman, my roommate. I thought it was wrong, I thought it was the worst thing I could have done to myself, and so I felt convicted, and I kept it to myself. We really liked each other, but it wasn't the right time. Society, family was different back then and wasn't accepting of the lifestyle, and so we ended. I really like her, but she was afraid of her parents and I of mine. The rest is history," Tameko adds.

"Damn, that was a lot. Egypt, I haven't heard much from you. What do you think?" Alanna asks.

"I don't have an opinion. It's your life, Tameko. I just hope you know what you're doing. Women hurt women too."

"I know, and we've been careful with each other as well as others. We have been dating for almost a year now. She wanted to be sure about moving forward. She was in a bad situation two years ago. It didn't end well. After that, she just became turned off by with men," Tameko replies.

"It's been two years? And you didn't tell us?" Alanna's voice rises.

"Now I'm surprised. A whole year, Tameko?" Egypt adds.

"And why haven't we been introduced to this woman yet?" Paris asks.

We met a year ago, it wasn't because I didn't want to. I was just waiting for the right time. And plus, I needed to feel secure about being with a woman. I still like men, but for right now, this is where am. I don't know about the rest of my life, but in this moment, it feels right. But what I need to know is that I have your respect and support—as my sisters and my family," Tameko says nervously. She thinks, *I'm in too deep, I can't turn back now.* This love thang is crazy!

"If you need reassurance, you've got it," Egypt responds. "Just don't rub our noses in your escapades. I don't want to know the gory details of your freak nights."

"You got it." Tameko laughs.

"Yeah, neither do I. Maybe in far future we can set up a date night?" Paris adds.

"*Maybe they will, but I don't want to meet her at all. I'm not ready yet. A date night? Hell no,*" Alanna replies.

"What? Why?" Tameko turns around to meet Alanna's glance.

"Because it's not right, and I am not in support of this nonsense! You used to be heavy, strong about men. Now, you're telling me you like being with women. No! I don't think so."

"There you go being judgmental, Alanna!" Egypt states.

"I'm not judging. I am not in agreement with this whole episode of her life."

"I'm sorry you feel that way, Alanna. Because I've always been supportive of everything you wanted to do. So why can't you be here for me now?"

"If you were telling me you wanted to change careers, relocate, have a threesome with men, or something like that . . . I would be supportive. But this takes it to a whole new level. This . . . it's not right, and I'm not ready to accept you being a les . . . " Alanna trails off, unable to even say the word.

"You mean GAY, LESBIAN, HOMOSEXUAL! SAY IT! THAT'S WHAT YOU THINK I AM!" Tameko yells.

"WHATEVER! I AM NOT ABOUT TO ARGUE WITH YOU OVER MY VIEW. I AM ABOUT TO LEAVE. ARE YOU WOMEN COMING OR NOT?" Alanna yells.

*"Ladies, for the record, I am not lesbian, gay, homosexual, or any of those things. I am just me, and I happened to be in love with this woman. I may eventually go back to men, but for right now, this is me! Alanna, please don't go. I want to continue talking with you. This is important to me."* Tameko walks behind them. *"WAIT! Don't go. I haven't finished talking with you. Please stay!"* Tameko tries to reason with them as they all walk out of the apartment.

"Egypt turns back...Tameko, they are in shock right now. Let them calm down, and we'll talk later in the week,".

"But I really wanted you to meet my girl. Or lease have a conversation with her. " Tameko adds.

"And we will, but not right now, I think it's time to go, and we can catch up later. Maybe for that drink?"

"NO, PLEASE . . . I AM SORRY. I DON'T WANT TO HURT YOU. I LOVE YOU. YOU'RE MY FAMILY. PLEASE!"

"It's a lot to take in at one time, Tam . . . that's all. We're not mad. Just surprised," Egypt adds.

"PARIS . . . WHY AREN'T YOU SAYING ANYTHING?" Alanna yells.

"Honestly, I am lost for words. This took me by surprise. I wasn't expecting this."

"HOW COULD YOU STAND THERE AND NOT DEFEND ME, PARIS? YOU KNOW MY HISTORY," Tameko exclaims.

"I never thought," Paris says. "I am sorry, Tam, I got to go. I'll call you later."

They all leave the apartment, and Tameko is left standing at the door as it closes.

# I AM IN TOO DEEP – CAN'T TURN BACK NOW!

You ever been into someone so hard you can't breathe? Just the
thought of them never being a part of your life is unthinkable.
Just the thought of them moving two steps or even
leaving you for a moment seems too long, I know.
It is in those rare moments when the intensity becomes to so
raw where the pretense of what that looks like is unfinished.
It's like Michelle and Barack, Bonnie and Clyde, Chicken George
and Matilda, a feeling that is only familiar to you. A knowing
that walking away is not an option because we're in too deep.
Living inseparable where only the essence of who
you are is their unfinished memory.
A fleet of words, a thought, which only
you knew before I thought them
A place where my heart penetrates your soul and
pierces so deep that only I could fill it.
My feet are placed directly next to yours, and my legs will
walk with you no matter where you go. I will ride with you,
die with you, I am here only for your eyes to see and my body
as your road map to draw upon, connect me with you, forging
towards eternity, as I am in too deep, and I can't turn back.

# THIS LOVE THANG

*Time has passed, and it's been a while since we've seen each other or talked with Tameko. I think it's time we gave her a call. Let me check in with the ladies and see how everyone is feeling,* Paris thinks.

She gets on the phone with Egypt. "Hey, girl, how are you? It's been a while."

"Yes, it's been about three weeks. I am so glad you called. I was thinking about how we left things. We were judging her decisions and not really giving her a chance to let us know she feels. We didn't handle that well," Paris states.

"I admit, we can all be extremely hard on each other at times, but this is our friend, the friend we promised to always be there for despite the bullshit. I think we should all go over there and talk with her. It's not like she killed someone," Egypt adds.

"I was thinking the same thing. I agree we didn't handle that right. It's her life, and we're family. Let me give Alanna a call," Paris responds.

"Hey, Egypt." Alanna answers. "What's up. Is there something wrong?"

"No, nothing is wrong," Egypt responds. "We wanted to know if you wouldn't mind going with us over to Tameko's place."

"I figured that's why you're calling. Who is the WE? Is Paris going too?"

"Yes. She is."

"Why now? Y'all feeling guilty?"

"US?" Egypt says in a high voice. "You're the one who should be feeling guilty after the way *you* treated her."

"EXCUSE ME? I have nothing to feel guilty about. I stated my business. I don't like her choices lately, but you're right. It's her life."

"Yes . . . it is."

"Look, I am only going because your ass is going," Alanna adds.

"Well, don't let us pull your leg." Egypt chuckles.

"Look, I am still not in agreement with her lifestyle, but I do want her to know that we're all here for her no matter what," Alanna states.

"Okay then. Let's go over there at seven o'clock tonight. I already called her and told her we would be stopping by," Egypt says.

"Oh, you did, did you?" Alanna responds. "You are so sneaky, Egypt."

"Yeah, well . . . where is Paris?"

"She'll meet us there. I'll meet you at your place at six-thirty—your ass be ready! You're the slowest one in the bunch."

"I'll be ready . . . bye!" Alanna hangs up.

\*\*\*

The girls arrive. "Paris, do you still have the key?" Egypt asks as they walk up to Tameko's apartment. "I left mine."

"Of course. I do," Paris answers.

As the girls enter the apartment, the lights are off, but music is playing slow and soft.

"Is that Monifah? 'Lay with You.' That's my shit . . . why is the lights off?"

"Hey." There appears to be light coming from the bedroom. Egypt notices.

"Tameko knew we were coming, didn't she?" Alanna whispers. "So why are all the lights out? We can hardly see ourselves."

"Tameko, are you here?" Paris softly calls out.

"Maybe no one is here. It seems she may have left. Let's go. I don't like the dark," Egypt responds.

"I know." Paris chuckles.

"Then why would there be music be playing and candles lit? Knowing Tameko's paranoid ass, she wouldn't have left the candles burning. I thought I saw her purse on the kitchen table. Maybe she forgot we were coming over," Egypt adds.

As the women begin to turn around and walk out, Tameko walks out of the bedroom half-dressed and startled. "What are you guys doing here?" she squeaks.

"Why are we here?" Alanna responds.

"We came over to see how you are. You *did* know we were stopping by, didn't you?" Paris asks.

"Oh sorry, I thought I still had a least an hour. I lost track of time."

"Oh yeah? Doing what?" Egypt says with a smirk. "Is there someone here?

"Yes, about that . . . " Tameko says, but she stops when she hears someone come out of the bedroom.

"Hi, I didn't know we were having company, babe. Hi, my name is—" the woman begins.

Paris looks up in surprise. "OH, HELL NO! This can't be the woman you're sleeping with and seeing."

"Why? You two know each other?" Egypt and Alanna state in unison. Alanna sneakily punches Egypt's arm.

"Hi, Paris!" The woman responds. "It's been a while."

"Wait. You know each other?" Tameko looks at Paris and then back to Sam.

"YES, THIS IS THE WOMAN I CAUGHT WITH JOH," Paris states.

"Biatch, don't act like we're old friends." Paris turns to her friends. "This is the woman I told y'all about. She was the one I caught in the bed with my man!"

"TAMEKO, DID YOU KNOW ABOUT THIS?" Alanna says. "You better start talking."

"Not at first, but once we got to know each other, she told me she was dealing with this brother, and once I figured out who it was, it was too late, and I was all in. It was too late. I didn't mean for you to find out like this, Paris . . . I . . ."

"YOU KNEW AND YOU DIDN'T SAY ANYTHING. THIS GIRL HURT ME IN THE WORST WAY. THIS SHIT ALMOST KILLED ME, SERIOUSLY!"

"Yes, but I . . . "

"BUT I WHAT? YOU ONLY THOUGHT OF YOUR FEELINGS AS USUAL, TAMEKO!" Alanna yells.

"YES, BUT AS YOUR FRIEND . . . YOU COULD'VE TOLD ME, CALLED ME, OR SAID SOMETHING TO ME," Paris says.

"THAT'S SOME FOUL SHIT. EVEN FOR YOU, TAMEKO!" Alanna states.

Egypt sticks out her hand to shake Samantha's, but Paris slaps it back. "No, you will not shake her hand or even speak to her!"

"I can see you're still very upset with me," Samantha states.

"UPSET WITH YOU! BIATCH, I WANTED TO BEAT YOUR ASS. I AM NOT JUST UPSET! I WANTED TO DRAG YOU. YOU WERE IN MY BED, IN MY HOUSE, AND WITH MY MAN AND YOU'RE STANDING THERE WITH A SMIRK ON YOUR FACE."

"I don't know what to say," Sam says.

"YOU REALLY THINK WE CAN BE FRIENDS AFTER WHAT I KNOW ABOUT YOU?" Paris responds. She begins to take off her coat and place her bag down. "YOU KNOW WHAT? YOU NEED TO COME GET THIS ASS-WHOOPING THAT I OWE YOU."

"GIRLLL, DON'T GET IT TWISTED. I MAY BE SMALL, BUT I WILL BUST YOUR ASS. Now, I apologized to you so many times before. I told you I didn't know about you."

"I don't care about your apology, and I don't give two shits about you!"

"YOU GOT THE AUDACITY TO THINK WE COULD ALL BE FRIENDS. SERIOUSLY! GET AWAY FROM ME!"

"I . . . I know you're still upset, but I am . . ."

"LADIES, THERE WILL BE NO ASS-WHOOPING here tonight," Egypt interjects.

"Paris, that is your name, right?

"Let me just smack the shit out of this . . . " Paris says.

"I'm going to say this one last time—I'm sorry," Samantha says. "I didn't know. Joh never told me about you, and I never knew he was in a relationship either. I learned it all when you came home that day and walked in."

"YEAH RIGHT! ALL WOMEN KNOW. DON'T TRY AND PLAY ME," Paris continues to yell.

*She turns her back to Paris. "I'm done with this conversation. So these are the women you were talking about, Tam?" Sam calmly says.*

"REALLY . . . SO YOU THINK YOU CAN TURN YOUR BACK TO ME? I AM ABOUT TO—" Paris yells.

"PARIS . . . STOP! LET HER TALK," Alanna says.

*Tameko turns around to Samantha. "Stop! This is my family. We've all been friends for far too long, and I am sorry. Honestly, I didn't put two and two together immediately. You never said her name, Paris. How was I supposed to know it was the same Samantha?"*

"I got to go," Paris states.

"I'm sorry too. The reason we came over was to apologize for the other night and to talk about who this mysterious woman is. But I guess now we know," Alanna says.

"SURPRISE!" Samantha says weakly.

"Girl . . . you think this is a joke," Paris chimes in. "I have nothing else to say to you. I'm getting ready to leave."

"No. Paris, please stay! I owe you an apology too. I should have told you, but by the time I put everything together, I was caught up. HONESTLY, I DIDN'T WANT TO LOSE YOU, AND I COULDN'T LOSE HER. THE REALITY IS I BETRAYED BY BEST FRIEND, BUT I WASN'T READY TO LOSE MY GIRL."

"Tameko, you're going to have to make a choice. We all can't be girls. I can't stand this chick," Paris states.

"Let me say this you and the rest of ladies. I am not a homewrecker, and I did not break up your relationship. You keep blaming me, but I did nothing wrong. This will be the last time I apologize to you," Samantha states.

"I know this hurts right now," Egypt adds, "but if she's telling the truth . . . it's not her fault. Now can we all calm down and just talk?"

"I guess we got the shock of our lives," Alanna observes. "The phone was off, and we decided to come over, otherwise we would've just met at the Thirst Monkey."

As Tameko proceeds to put the phone back on the hook, she continues with her explanation. "Honestly, when I tried to tell you I was seeing a woman and that I was a lesbian, I knew you wouldn't be ready to hear it. Especially since the person was Samantha."

"I guess you're right. I wouldn't have not been receptive," Paris responded.

I don't want to hurt you, Paris, you my best friend but now...

"Tam, baby, I don't want you to have to choose anyone. I am just going to pack my things. I'll be leaving now. It's looks like you ladies got some things to talk about," Samantha says.

"Yeah . . . why don't you do that!" Paris exclaims.

"NO, WAIT! Samantha! We need to work this out because she's not going anywhere because this is where she belongs, with me!"

"Okay, then I guess that's it," Egypt adds.

"The last time I checked this was our house, and I decide who is going and who is staying. Now if you want to leave, Paris, you can! I love you, but don't make me have to choose."

"YOU'RE THROWING ME OUT?" Paris responds.

"No! I am not, but if you want to leave. I won't try to stop you." Tameko turns around to Sam. "I love this girl. And this is who I am with."

"Really! No worries. I am leaving," Paris says.

*Egypt suddenly changes the subject.* "No, seriously! How did you two women meet anyway?"

"Yes! It's about to get hot up in here," Alanna chimes in.

"Well, if you must know, we met at Candy Girls—a strip club in New Jersey," Samantha says. "She asked me for a lap dance, and I obliged."

"Did y'all know I used to be a stripper?" Tameko asks.

"WHAT?" the girls say in unison.

"Yes, I used to strip back in my college days. It paid for school. It was what we had in common. And the rest is history."

"Cliché, I might add." Alanna chuckles.

"As we were getting to know each other, we found out we had a lot in common. Honestly, this was not my first rodeo with women, but this one I chose to be serious with."

"As for me," Samantha adds, "after Joh, I was done with men. He hurt me as well. I'm not that woman. I wouldn't knowingly do that to another woman."

"You can do better than her," Paris says as she turns to Tameko.

"DO BETTER? WHAT IS THAT SUPPOSED TO MEAN, Paris?" Samantha asks.

"Paris, I think you're doing too much," I'm not in agreement of this whole new lifestyle for Tameko, but you are going too far. Alanna says.

"I know you're mad, and I don't blame you, but you're angry at the wrong person. Furthermore, I'm not going to be called a whore in my own house," Samantha replies.

"YOUR HOUSE?" Paris asks.

"Yes, Samantha moved in with me yesterday," Tameko says with a smile. "That was why I wanted us to meet tonight, but you came a little earlier than I expected."

"Well, you better be careful before she cheats on you," Paris warns.

"I'm not going to cheat on her," Samantha responds. "I truly love Tameko. Besides, you're the one who should make sure your man doesn't cheat on you again. I understand you're back together?"

"WHAT? How do you know about my business?" Paris's voice heightens.

"Tameko and I talked, and you don't have to worry. I don't want him," Samantha finishes dryly. "He already knows how I taste . . . anyway! This love thang is crazy. Isn't it?"

Paris wipes her lips. "For the record, we're better than ever!"

"Girl, glad, I could help." Samantha chuckles.

"Hey, hey, stop it, ladies," Egypt interjects. "This is so unnecessary."

"Just keep this heifer away from me," Paris says. "I don't trust her."

"You don't have to like or love her, but you will respect her," Tameko responds. "She's with me and I'm with her. We live together now! Paris, please stop this. Don't make me have to choose."

"I think it's best we all give back our keys then." Egypt smirks. "I guess there will be no more walking in on them anymore."

"My stomach is sick," Paris responds. "Here are your keys and the rest of your life. I hope you two are *happy* with each other."

As the women prepare to leave, they all embrace. "Listen," Paris says, "you are my girls for life—but not her." She shoots a look at Samantha.

"You gonna have to get used to it, Paris. Sam is here to stay," Tameko says.

"JUST WAIT FOR IT!" Paris yells back as she walks out the door. Tameko walks out behind them. "Babe, I'll be right back."

"I don't think your friends will ever accept me. Especially Paris, with the history of Joh between us. Like I said, I'll leave if you want me to," Samantha states.

"No, this is not about my friends, family, or anybody else . . . just the woman I love. I know them. They'll come around sooner or later. We're family."

***

Paris walks into the elevator and turns to Egypt and Alanna.

"She is going to be a constant reminder that Joh cheated on me. I can't stand that girl," she exclaims. "She was in bed with my man! To walk in on something like that . . . it hurts! And you never forget something like that. And now, SHE IS WITH MY BEST FRIEND. TAMEKO WANTS TO BRING HER AROUND IN FRONT OF THE FAMILY AND BE ALL 'KUMBAYA' . . . I DON'T THINK SO. NOPE! NO WAY!"

Ladies wait. I need to say something to you. Paris, please.

What do you want Tameko, you already embarrass me with this news of yours?

I wanted you know that I love of you and we can do this together. Just be open. Tameko ask

Alanna responds first. "Paris, Joh cheated on you with her. He took her to your home. It's not entirely her fault. Furthermore, if she didn't know, then how can you blame her? Be easy! Like Tameko said, whether you're okay with it or not, they are moving forward with their relationship."

"Not with *that* tramp!" Paris replies. "Out of all the women, she chose her!"

"I don't think it was a choice. They just happened to work at the same place. This world is small. Love happens when it happens." Alanna adds.

***

"Let's give it a minute and set up another day to talk. I am sure we can work things out. Remember, we're not just friends. We're family," Egypt says.

I am open to that. I got to go to the movies with my girl. Talk to you later. Tameko replies.

"I don't want to be in the same room as her!" Paris exclaims. "That day almost destroyed me! Tameko knew the damage it caused. Now it feels like Sam is acting like she doesn't even care."

"Why do you say that?" Egypt asks.

"The minute Tam knew it was her, she should've walked away. Especially since I told her about the situation. I don't understand why she even considered dating her or whatever."

"Tameko loves this woman. You can't help who you love, Paris. You know this. Isn't that why you went back to Joh?

EXCUSE ME? You throw that in my face!

Besides, I don't hear you blaming Joh. He is the real culprit here, and I know you too are considering getting back together, so if you can forgive him, then you surely can look past Sam."

"I don't know," Paris replies.

Egypt reasons, "Tameko wants to be with her with or without your blessing, Paris. Look, we're all going out tonight to get some drinks. Do you want to go out or what? If not, I'm going home." This love thang is confusing.

"Then, take y'all asses home. I want to be alone right now!"

"See that's that - bullshit: always walking away. I can't stand your ass sometimes. You can be *so* rude."

"This shit got me vexed right now, and I can't talk anymore. I need to think. Here, read this shit for the road."

Hey before we go, you always leave us with a Poem. Can we get one.

No, this one is in my head. I going to recite it to myself on my way home, good night. I can't.

# THIS LOVE THANG

Sometimes the hardest walk is the journey of love. There
are so many levels to loving and when I think who, why,
when it is with you. I've never loved the way this way before;
it feels so good and I want it to last forever. In my heart, it
feels like everlasting love shared between two people.
Simply put, I want this love thang for as long as I can have it. Take
my hand and I guide my love, share my thoughts as I try to penetrate
yours. I can't seem to shake this feeling, but I want it stay with me.

This love thang takes me back to Michelle and Barack, Bonnie
and Clyde, and Chicken George and Matilda, where timeless love
defeats the roads traveled. The day you grab my hand, telling me
to walk with that if I can trust your heart, I can be safe forever.

The path of our love is forever moving I just want to be where
you are. Following your path, step by step, if we do it together.
I don't want to be with anyone else, and I can't resist this love
thang we got going on. I don't question what we have, and I
never wish to be anywhere else. I am in awe of what this love
brings. Aiming to bridge the gaps that follow, engulf all of
what this offers. I am forever caught up in this love thang.

# WHO WE LOVE!

"Hi, it's been a few days since we've spoken," Alanna begins. "I thought I would give you a call Paris, because when you get in your feelings, you ignore folks."

"What do you want?" Paris replies. "I'm still mad. I don't feel like talking."

"It's been a minute since the last time we were all together," Alanna continues, "I called Tameko. Now that the cards are on the table, I know this is not what you want to hear, but she isn't going to change her mind."

"Don't you think I know that? I don't have a problem with Tameko's sexuality or who she loves—just this particular person. I wish it had been someone else, that's all. This is not what I expected."

"Well, what you don't know is Tameko and Samantha share a lot in common. They were both jilted by men, stripping, and you, Paris."

"Do I look I am joking right now? Alanna, dang."

"I wasn't trying to be funny. Girl, just listen for a minute. Tameko told me when she was out there dating, she was dying inside. She wanted someone to love her for herself. She wasn't being fulfilled by men anymore. Samantha was there, and she saved her life."

"What do you mean saved her life?" Paris asks.

"Honestly, Tameko was contemplating suicide."

"WHAT? No, not Tameko!"

"She couldn't handle the loneliness any longer, and Samantha came along and rescued her."

"I never knew that," Paris says.

"I know," Alanna responds. "She wanted you and everyone to think everything was okay, but it wasn't. She didn't want anyone to know her pain. Since then, I've had a change of heart too. Honestly, I am not in agreement with this lifestyle, but it's her choice, and I'm not going stand in her way. Life is too short for crap. I'd rather have Tameko in my life than live without her. I'm happy for Tameko. I am. We can't help who we love."

"I know that's right," Paris says. "Hell, look at you and Massai. I never thought you two would end up with each other."

"And of course, I never thought you'd go back to Joh, but you did."

"Touché, biatch. I guess I will give her call. I just need a minute. This shit is too real, and it hurts no matter how you cut the mustard," Paris adds.

"I know you felt betrayed, but the betrayal was not with Samantha. I don't need to recall the whole incident, but I will tell you this: we waste a lot of time blaming our stuff on other people, but the truth is we have to first look at ourselves. In the end, you can't help who you fall in love with. It just happens."

"I know that, and I know I am being too hard on Tameko, but Samantha though. Ugh, I can't," Paris answers.

"You can, you *will,* or you *will* lose Tameko," Alanna states.

I understand now. I guess I need to get over myself and learn to accept it.

Now, you sound like with sister we all know and love.

Listen the first time that biatch tries to say anything sarcastic, I am really going slap the shit out of her.

"I believe you, but I don't think she wants re-live that incident either. It hurt her just as much. So, let it go Paris and move forward, with that being said you know I need one of them poems for the road."

I know and here it goes…who we love!

## WHO WE LOVE!

*I know I shouldn't, but I can't help but want to*
*When I see you, all I want to do is touch, kiss you*
*But you seem so far away, and yet you're standing right next to me*
*Some might say you're not mine to have, and yet I want to anyway*
*I wait for the moment to walk down the street*
*with you, to be in a place where eyes*
*That wonder will no longer care. I wait to kiss your face and know*
*that is okay. I can't breathe when you're not around, and I wait for the*
*moment when you're here with me in the same room, a place where only*
*you and I share. It's a place of peace for only for a moment. Where no*
*one can have anything to say. Because I can't help who I love. I can't*
*help that it is with you, and I promise to wait. Yes, I will wait for you*
*for as long as you want, even if it feels like an eternity. I am totally*
*in love with you, and the presence of who are to me is everything.*

# AT LAST I LOVE!

Paris hears a knock at the door. "Here goes that shit again. I am going to have to really speak with management. Security is not taking me seriously. There is a reason why I pay for amenities. I want my phone call first. Damn!" Paris yells, "Who is it?"

"It's me, Egypt. Open the door. Girl, it's been a week. Can I come in?"

"Where is security? He should have called me first, and I would have told him not to let you in."

"Really? Biatch, Maybe he went to the gentlemen's room or at lunch. It is after 1:00 p.m." It ain't that serious.

"What do you want? I only got five minutes. I was headed out to the store."

"What's up? We haven't heard from you since you, the girls, and I met up with Tam and Samantha last week."

"I'm having a hard time with this whole situation. The same woman who cheats with my man is now sleeping my best friend—and they're in love! Can you believe this shit?! I don't know how I can even stomach it or even remain friends with Tameko," Paris says angrily.

"Joh cheated on you with Sam—not the other way around. I came over here to try and talk sense into your ass. You're so mad at Samantha, you've forgotten she's innocent in all this."

"How can she be innocent?" Paris says.

"All I'm saying is, she didn't know about you and Joh. You may not want to hear this, but that one is on Joh. Samantha seems genuinely sorry, not to mention Tam and Sam seem to be into one another. Tameko is finally in love! Do you want to be the one to destroy that? No judgment, remember? We've all done things we're not proud of."

"I know. It's just that she'll always be around to remind me of Joh's infidelity," Paris says somberly.

"You can't throw it in her face every time you see her. I mean Joh's infidelity," Egypt says.

"I know and I'm embarrassed."

"What do you have to be embarrassed about? He did the cheating. It had nothing to do with your womanhood. He was being a greedy and irresponsible. Just like most. This world is small," Egypt finishes with a laugh.

"I don't find this shit funny right now," Paris responds.

"Paris, I'm not laughing at you, but you got to admit, it is somewhat funny. Listen, I gotta go. I'll talk to you later. Love ya." Egypt prepares to leave when she hears a knock at the door. "Paris, are you expecting someone?"

"No, but the security guard is fired tomorrow!" Paris states.

"I'm leaving but you need to make up with Tameko. You are miserable!" Egypt exits.

"Not!" Paris responds.

Egypt opens the door. Samantha is standing at the entrance.

"Hi, lady . . . " She begins to walk past Egypt. "I need to need to speak with Paris, now! Is she here?"

"What the hell are you doing at my house? How did you get past security? No one called to tell me you were downstairs or that someone wanted to come up," Paris states.

"No one was downstairs. Maybe he went to the bathroom or something.

A lot of that going around lately, Egypt smirks.

"I believe we need to talk."

"And what the hell do we need to talk about?"

"Well on that note," Egypt says, "I'm going to leave you two ladies alone. I got to go the supermarket before it closes. Good night, ladies . . .

don't try to kill each other." Egypt walks out the door, but Samantha still doesn't enter Paris's home.

"I don't want to talk to you," Paris says. "And how do you know where I live? Oh wait . . . I forgot. YOU were already here and in my bed."

Samantha ignores the snide remarks. "I came over to speak with you, woman to woman. We need to put this shit behind us if we're going to be traveling in the same group together.

Does she know you're here?

Yes, Tameko knows I am here. Can I come in?"

"I'm not sure if I want a womanizer or a criminal in my house. I have a lot of valuables here."

"Girl please, you're going too far. You have nothing I want. Again! Can I come inside? You got me standing in the hallway like some delivery person. What I have to say will not take long."

"Come in," Paris responds.

"I came here because of Tameko, so let me say what I need to say, then I'll go."

"Okay. Go ahead. You got five minutes."

"I can see how much you mean to Tameko, and that goes the same for her, and she means just as much to me. This has got to stop. I can't keep fighting with you. It hurts Tameko."

"I don't know what you want me to say. You got three minutes. It's getting late," Paris states.

"Girl, it's four in the afternoon. Listen, this may sound like a broken record, but for the last time, if Joh had told me he was in a relationship, it wouldn't have happened," Samantha adds.

"Really?" Paris says with a raised eyebrow.

"Yes. Really. I'm here on the strength of Tameko. *This* is really bothering her. I am not willing to step in between family and friends. She means too much to me. I'll walk away. We have a year, but you've had a lifetime with her."

"And your point is?"

"The point is . . . that this isn't for everyone, but its right for us. I hope in time, you can find your way to forgive me. I hope we can work it out."

"Try later than sooner," Paris responds.

"Anyhoo . . . I am asking for you to give us a chance for Tameko," Samantha states.

"Well, I can see you really love my girl. But don't ask for too much all at once. I'm not ready to accept you into the family."

"I understand. Truth be told, I don't like you either, but maybe one day, we can share a laugh together."

"At whose expense?" Paris responds. "Mine?"

"As long as you see yourself as the victim, you will be. But hey, I gotta go."

As Samantha starts to walk out, she turns to Paris. "I love Tameko! She's happy and so am I. In the end, life is about finding your heart's true desire. Life is too short for drama and nonsense. At last, we finally found love in each other."

"Okay, Ms. Thing. I hear you. Oh, and don't be coming to my house unexpected in the future. Next time, call or I'm going have to call the police!"

"Girl, really! I thought your fake security cop was your protection. Like I said, he must've gone to the gentlemen's room. Everybody gotta piss sometimes. You are taking this shit way to the left, for no reason."

"Yeah. Whatever. Bye, biatch!"

Samantha is about to leave but turns around. "Hey . . . I am no one's biatch. I told you that before. If we're going to work through this . . . you're going have to stop calling me out of my name."

"Respect. My apologies," Paris states.

"We can start right now. My name is Samantha Jones."

"Excuse me. What is your name? You said Jones."

"Yes."

"That's funny, my last name is Jones too. Where are you from?"

"I am from Detroit originally."

"So am I!"

"Oh really . . . and who's your daddy?" Sam asks.

"Michael Jones? Wait, he got a tattoo on the left side of his neck, and he served in the Marines but got discharged for some nonsense. They threw him out," Paris says.

"Yes, mine too!" Sam turns around.

"HE'S FROM THE SOUTHSIDE!" they both shout.

"NOPE . . . NO, NO! This can't be . . ." Paris walks away and returns, stating, "YOU CAN'T BE . . . . MY . . ." Paris screams.

# *AT LAST I LOVE!*

*When the time comes to love*
*It chooses you. Choosing to love is what*
*Most people want, but sometimes they never*
*Have the opportunity to really experience it. Does it really matter? Or does*
*love become the commodity?*
*Having someone who will stand with and for you is our only desire to say*
*At last I love!*
*It chose me to love, and it gave me the chance to give back without conditions*
*Or expectations. I am in love now, and I am completely in awe of what love*
*Feels like to me. The imprint it leaves on my body, and the fragrances that*
*explode in my nose from the scent and taste of your love.*
*The sweat that runs down my face, while running to meet you in a space*
*where only you and I would know. I embrace this without knowing the*
*outcome. I do not want to hold back, I just want you to know, at last I love,*
*it's my journey to love you back!*

# NOTES

# MY FINAL THOUGHT

*This Love Thang,* the first poetry novel, is about eleven friends on the path to accepting, finding, and forgiving love in their eyes. Each poem and chapter signify their voice, feelings, and expression of what love is. Will the path they've all chosen be too much even for them to handle? She's a poet, he's a momma's boy, she is on the path to self-destruction, will curiosity kill the cat? He must grow up, he doesn't listen, he is a nightmare waiting to happen, she is mischievous, and she is the best-kept secret.

**Love** . . . is a conversation that many people love to have. It's often between friends, seeking love and searching to find its true destiny. ***This Love Thang,*** there're many roads traveled, but on this journey, friends help each other through their issues, teaching us valuable lessons about ourselves. Will the path taken be the hardest road to travel? Is love easy or hard to obtain? You tell me!

It signifies the journey each one has taken in lieu of finding love and maintaining friendships. Where there is a path, lessons are learned. In each situation, they discover things about one another they have never known. Inside their sister circle and men's club, can all be forgiven, or should they just let sleeping dogs lie?

Printed in the United States
By Bookmasters